NOTHING MORE THAN ZERO

Book 1 of The Dragon's Honor Series

C. H. Smith

Swamp Island Words

For all those that escape to other worlds in the pages of a book...

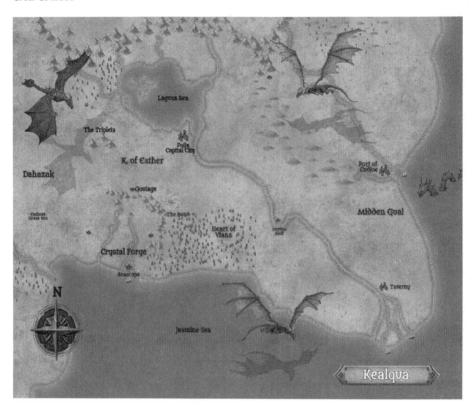

CHAPTER 1

The empty quiver dangled from Jaxson's sweaty back as he scanned the southern and western sky for any still in pursuit. He and his dragon, both exhausted, could see for miles from the top of this ridge. To the east, the sun had finally crested the tallest of the peaks in the Dragon's Spine. To the north lay uncharted territory.

"Think we finally lost them," he said, still searching the skies.

It had been a long night attempting to evade the large group of steam drakes. Zero would have no problem taking on a single drake, or even four, but they had been pursued by multiple dozens at least. Their long, slender bodies were built for bursts of speed. Jaxson had never known of this many eagle-sized drakes working together, and their sustained pursuit wasn't typical of their hunting style.

"Let me have a look at that wing," Jaxson said to Zero. "You keep your eyes sharp."

Zero extended his left wing as he gazed south, watching for any sign of the drakes. It didn't take Jaxson long to find the slash in the thin membrane between the long bones of Zero's wing. There was very little blood, and the cut was straight. *Thank the tiny gods for that,* thought Jaxson as he rummaged through his pack, looking for something to mend the wound.

As he finished sewing up his dragon's wing with a fish hook and line, he noticed a pool of blood around one of Zero's back legs.

"Oi, what happened there?"

"What happened where?" asked Zero in Jaxson's thoughts.

"Your back leg is all bloody! Did you not notice that?"

Zero swung his barrel-sized head around to see for himself. "*So it is,*" he said in Jaxson's mind, before turning his attention back to the south and west.

"And when did that happen? You been bleeding all night?" asked Jaxson.

Zero allowed him to tend the wound but offered no further insight into the cause of the injury. He just kept sentry, waiting for the relentless steam drakes to appear.

After mending the wound as best he could, Jaxson leaned on a rock overlooking the valley that wasn't the same valley he had spent most of his life in. After years of waiting for word from his father without a clue to his whereabouts, an old man, Dreknoxious, had shown up at his door with a hint of where to look. They had agreed to travel together to the Kingdom of Esther, but on the way, Dreknoxious had departed on urgent business. He promised to return and help their other traveling companion, the Princess of Seascape, face a fearsome battle. Jaxson decided to help too.

It was in that battle, facing terrible odds, that Jaxson and Zero fought against the Goat Head Sorcerer for the Princess. The steam drakes, vast in number, had forced Jaxson and Zero to flee the field. As long as the drakes were pursuing them, they couldn't fight alongside the Princess's army. But unlike other steam drakes, this horde did not get bored and give up. They had pursued Jaxson and Zero through the mountains and the night. Jaxson knew that he and Zero needed to find a place to rest safely, but this was unfamiliar territory. To the south, he thought he could see the triple peaks that towered over the Red Dragon Castle. That would place them almost at the point where the mountain range swept west and dangerously close to the Bend.

His father had taken great care in warning Jaxson about the strange things that occurred this far north. Creatures straight out of legends and nightmares roamed the mountains and the skies. An unnatural sea storm swirled over the land constantly, never moving away. The high winds from the storm spun out menacing clouds and frequent lightning. It was no place for man or dragon. Jaxson told Zero they had best avoid going farther north.

"*We need to find shelter and get some rest,*" said Zero in Jaxson's thoughts.

Aloud, Jaxson responded, "Yeah, we do... first time we leave the comfort of our little valley, and all this happens."

Zero looked at him and chuckled. "*At least it's not boring.*"

They both laughed. Jaxson's shoulders relaxed, and he rolled his head in large circles. Eyes closed, he felt the adrenaline seep away and weariness start to take over.

CHAPTER 2

The sun burned through Jaxson's eyelids, forcing him out of his deep sleep. He shook his head slowly to clear it, then looked out over the valley. The ground was rocky beneath him, and he could feel the rhythmic, deep breaths of Zero at his back.

Suddenly, his eyes widened. They should not have slept in the open, exposed.

He bolted to his feet and screamed for Zero to wake up. His head jerked from side to side as he searched the skies.

Zero rose quickly, though he stifled a yawn.

"How could we be so stupid?" said Jaxson.

Zero did not respond, but only moved to the edge of the ridge.

"Do you see anything?" asked Jaxson. His eyes were still wide and his hands had yet to calm. He shuddered at the thought of what would have happened if the steam drakes had found them in so vulnerable a position.

"I do not see pursuit from the south or west," said Zero.

Jaxson's shoulders relaxed, and his hands stopped quaking so violently. "Thank all the tiny gods... Maybe we lost them for good."

His gaze shifted to the east. He half-expected to see a wall of steam drakes bearing down on them, but all he saw were blue skies and a lone eagle riding the current of the wind. The noble one circled high above, either in search of a meal or just enjoying the wind through his feathers. Seeing this was a good omen, and Jaxson liked good omens.

A small smile crept onto his face. It had been a long and

frightful night, and there had been several moments when he had been sure the steam drakes would be their end. In the warm light of day, however, watching the noble eagle own the skies above him, a sense of peace overcame him. He was on his way to find his long overdue father. Thanks to the old man, Dreknoxious, he even had a place to begin searching.

His smile faltered as he thought of the old man. They had intended to travel to the capital of the Kingdom of Esther together. Circumstances Jaxson did not fully understand had caused Dreknoxious to depart quickly with only a promise to return. Jaxson had no idea how the old man would find him now, after their terror-filled flight through the mountains. *But if anyone can find me, it's him,* thought Jaxson.

He was brought out of his daydream by a strange grating sound. He looked all around but could not see anything that might have caused the noise. Zero had not seemed to notice, his gaze still locked on the horizon. Jaxson thought he might have imagined the whole thing, until he heard it again. The sounds of large rocks scraping together was closer this time, coming from on top of the ridge above them. Jaxson walked towards the sound and noticed a large, crevice concealed by a slight rise. The sound stopped just as Jaxson peered over the edge, down into the dark. The deep shadows concealed everything beyond a few feet. He nudged a small stone off the edge and heard it strike the wall on the way down. He waited patiently, expecting it to hit the bottom at any moment.

"*There is movement to the south,*" said Zero.

Jaxson didn't respond, still staring into the inky black darkness. He waited for the sound to come again; in each moment that passed a tiny trickle of fear filled more of him. A strange thought tickled the back of Jaxson's mind. *Something was down there.* Something darker than the deep crevice itself.

More urgently this time, Zero said, "*There is significant movement to the south, and it's headed our way.*"

Jaxson waved a hand, then bent closer to the crevice. He strained his eyes for any sign of movement.

"We need to go now!" said Zero in his mind.

Jaxson had started to turn away from the crack when he saw a blink.

"What the—" he yelled as a giant petridrake burst up from the crevice.

Pebbles and dust rained down as the gray drake rose high into the air, unfurling his wings and bellowing a fierce challenge. Zero was at Jaxson's side in an instant, urging him to mount. Jaxson only stared slack-jawed at the ancient beast. With skin rougher and harder than stone, the petridrake was larger than its cousins, the steam drakes. It was larger even than Zero. Still stunned, Jaxson watched as the beast locked eyes on Zero and started to dive.

Without hesitation, Zero sprung up to meet the attack. Jaxson recoiled from the shock of their impact that reverberated deep in his chest. The heavier petridrake drove Zero back towards the ridge. Fresh blood dripped from Zero's back leg and wing.

"Get away from it!" yelled Jaxson. He started running to the edge of the ridge. Zero wheeled from underneath the petridrake, skimming the rocky ground as he soared away from the immediate danger. Jaxson reached the end of the ridge and watched as Zero slowly gained altitude once more.

"I've got an idea," said Zero.

"Don't do anything crazy," said Jaxson. Even though the distance was great, Zero heard him and laughed.

"Watch this. Look south," the dragon said in Jaxson's thoughts.

Jaxson looked in that direction and saw their persistent pursuers, the steam drakes, approaching quickly.

Zero banked hard directly at the petridrake. The stone-skinned beast snarled and leapt towards Zero.

The moment before impact, Zero veered away. The petridrake shot past but recovered quickly to give chase. Zero led him towards the steam drakes, always staying just out of reach. Jaxson could do nothing but watch as his friend turned his head and blew dragon's fire towards the petridrake, then suddenly went into a sharp dive. The petridrake, temporarily blinded by the fire, kept due south – straight into the eager steam drakes.

The piercing cries of the steam drakes filled the air as they were forced to engage this new enemy. Zero, flying close to the mountains, circled back to the ridge undetected.

Jaxson climbed onto his back, and the pair made their escape. To the east laid the Heart of Viana, where men and dragons alike were rumored to enter and never return. West or south would mean risking an encounter with the victor of the steam drakes and the petridrake. The only option was north... towards the Bend.

CHAPTER 3

A gentle tailwind helped keep Zero aloft as the duo made their way slowly towards the Bend. The mountains below grew more hostile. There were no longer green trees or plants, or any other signs of life. Jaxson could see no place where they could land and rest comfortably.

At least the bleeding from his leg has stopped, and his wing is holding up, thought Jaxson.

"It is. I think I will be fine," Zero responded.

"I didn't realize I was talking to you," said Jaxson.

"No matter. You are exhausted. Let's rest."

"Not yet," Jaxson said, looking at the wall of clouds ahead.

Black, gray, and white clouds swirled. The vortex was an impenetrable barrier. Silent lightning from within the clouds flashed sporadically across the horizon. The unnatural storm, constantly spinning and dancing, never opened to reveal what lay beyond. Jaxson thought it looked angry.

Zero banked to the left, traveling parallel to the storm. Jaxson tore his eyes away from the clouds to look for a likely spot to rest. The jagged rocks below were uninviting. Still, he kept looking for a smooth stretch of ground or a nice overhang that would hide them while they recuperated. The empty quiver on his back reminded him how vulnerable they were out in the open.

"I don't believe it!" he said suddenly.

"What do you not believe?"

"Approaching from behind us," replied Jaxson.

A large group of steam drakes – albeit smaller than it once was – loped haggardly on their tail.

"*Will they ever give up?*" asked Zero.

Jaxson sighed. "We won't survive another encounter. There are just too many for you, and my bow is useless."

"*I see no other options,*" said Zero.

Despite Zero's best efforts, the steam drakes gained on them steadily until Jaxson could see the wounds from their battle with the petridrake. The charcoal-gray leader was missing one of his hot-ember-colored eyes. Several others had gashes or torn wings. They maintained pursuit relentlessly.

"Zero! They're getting close. Into the clouds..." said Jaxson. "It's our only chance."

Zero tensed beneath him, but hesitated only a moment before turning straight into the storm of the Bend. "*Hold on tight, Jaxson.*"

The storm pulled them in with amazing force. Jaxson's head was thrown back, and he struggled to remain in the harness. He gripped with both hands as his dark hair whipped into his face. Through the strands, he saw the remaining steam drakes follow them into the storm and promptly get obliterated, the wind hitting them with such force that they were torn apart. Jaxson would have smiled if it had been possible.

There was a tremendous pain in his head as if it was being smashed between large boulders until nothing existed except the sound of the wind and his tenuous hold on the harness. He couldn't hear Zero; he couldn't even hear himself think.

Then the hair on the back of his neck stood up. Zero tensed once more, his wings straining. A flash of blinding white light engulfed them, followed by the crushing sound of thunder. The hurricane continued to rage. So loud. Jaxson's hold on reality slipped. He attempted to call out to Zero, but no words came. His vision blurred. The pressure on his head was too much, and he slid slowly into the nothingness.

CHAPTER 4

Jaxson floated blissfully along in the deep nothing suspended in the inky darkness for an amount of time beyond reckoning. He had not heard any sound or seen anything at all in the comforting darkness. He was relaxed and free. He thought he heard something – a voice, perhaps. Then he heard it – really heard it, this time. Definitely a voice. He couldn't make out the words, but he was sure the voice was familiar.

A troubling thought occurred to him. *Where am I?* When nothing came to mind even as he strained his eyes and ears and racked his brain, he was disquieted for the first time in the dark. *Who am I?*

"*Jaxson! Jaxson! Are you well?*" screamed Zero across the black expanse.

As if swimming up from the depths of a warm pool, Jaxson followed the voice. Slowly at first, then with more urgency. His eyes blasted open and light flooded him, threatening to consume him just as the darkness had. He was dazed by the brilliance of a warm, sunny afternoon sky.

He blinked rapidly, and slowly his vision adjusted. A concerned Zero towered over him, but Jaxson barely saw him. Instead, the green, fertile valley took his full attention. Tall, evergreen trees lined the outer rim of the valley, giving way to large oaks. To the west, a rumbling waterfall cascaded from a mountain into a large pool, with several streams branching out. The sight of the falling water reminded Jaxson of his intense thirst. He stood up and, for the first time, he noticed the castle at the far side of the valley. It was huge, and Jaxson was drawn to it... drawn to a pulsing power coming from the ancient stones.

"Are you well?"

"I'm fine. Where are we?"

Zero took a long, slow look around the valley before he said, *"Within the storm."*

Again, Jaxson looked up at the blue sky. He was going to object, but then he noticed that above the mountains all around them swirled dark clouds. They were in the eye of the storm.

"That's odd."

"That is not all that is odd. Look up there," said Zero. He indicated the ridge just behind them. Sitting perfectly still, watching them, was a smokey dragon. It was twice as large as Zero, and even from this distance, Jaxson could tell something was off. The smoke dragon did not look solid. It shifted, and its edges were difficult to distinguish.

"How long has it been there?" asked Jaxson.

"I have been able to differentiate a total of three, and at least one has been visible at all times since we arrived. They fade in and out but have not come any closer."

"What do you think they want?" asked Jaxson.

Zero shrugged.

Jaxson looked back down into the valley. He had to make an effort not to look at the castle. Instead, he followed the path of the longest stream east across the valley floor. They needed water and something to eat. The stream passed through trees that he thought may bear fruit. He glanced back up at the smokey dragon. It faded away just as another started to take shape several feet away.

"Come on, let's go have a drink," said Jaxson as he climbed into the riding harness.

CHAPTER 5

He looked over his shoulder and was shocked to see not one smokey dragon but all three perched on the ridge behind them. Zero pushed off the ground with his powerful legs as he unfurled his wings. They were off. Jaxson smiled as the breeze hit his face. Again, he looked behind them. The smoke dragons were in pursuit but keeping their distance. One was directly behind and one on each side.

"We have company," said Jaxson.

Zero just snorted and kept flying at a leisurely pace.

"Head toward the waterfall."

Zero tried to angle to the west but was cut off by the smokey dragon on that side. He tried again and the dragon from the rear appeared, keeping them from turning.

"Let's try the other direction."

With a quick snap of his wings, Zero dove down and to the right, under the third smoke dragon. The rear dragon gave a piercing cry as all three turned quickly in pursuit, and then vanished. Jaxson looked over his shoulder but could no longer see any of the dragons.

"Nice move, Zero! They seem to have lost interest—"

Fire erupted in front of them. Jaxson could smell the heat as Zero turned sharply from the inferno. Through the flames and waves of heat, Jaxson saw all three smoke dragons billowing dragon's fire, creating a barrier not dissimilar to the clouds of the storm around the Bend. With no options left, Zero angled toward the structure in the distance and set a deliberately slow pace. Jaxson, still singed, did not like their destination being forced upon them but could think of no alternative.

The smoke dragons resumed their escort positions, appearing content to leave Jaxson and Zero alone if they flew in the direction they chose. As they approached the large structure, Jaxson could see more details. It resembled a castle, but everything seemed too large. The towers were easily twice as tall as any structure Jaxson had ever seen. The stones that made up the towers were jet black and as large as the mountain cottage he had called home for years.

"Land well before the gate," he said. "Let's get an idea of what we're getting into."

"You think the smoke dragons will allow that?"

"As long as we don't stray, I think they'll leave us be. They didn't bother us earlier."

"We'll see." Zero slowed and started a soft descent well before the large gate.

Just before Zero touched down, the smoke dragons disappeared. Jaxson dismounted and walked to Zero's head. Both stared at the immense structure in front of them. Seven tall towers shot up above a large central structure. It was encircled by a wall fifty feet high and just as thick, but the gate was what caught Jaxson's attention. It was as imposing and almost as tall as wall itself, with seven metal bars thicker than his legs. On each bar hung a huge sigil which appeared to have been carved with painstaking care. The top sigil depicted three small circles on the tracks of a larger circle within a larger circle still. Within each of the three smallest circles, detailed scenes were carved.

One such scene showed a king wearing a crown and with rings on all of his fingers. He was walking up a flight of stairs which were actually peasants bent over in varying degrees of supplication. Despite the distance between them and the gate, Jaxson had little trouble seeing and understanding the scene of the greedy king. The sigil slightly lower and to the left appeared at first to be simply a wavy line crossing the large metal circle. Then Jaxson noticed it wasn't a solid line. Instead, the flowing line was formed by naked, interlocking bodies. The details made Jaxson blush.

Each sigil was elegantly simple in design but intricate and precise in form. One showed an eye above a pyramid, and another depicted a five-pointed star created by jagged, sharp lines. There were others, and Jaxson tried to etch each one into his mind. They seemed powerful and important.

"Our guides are back," said Zero, bringing Jaxson back to situation at hand.

The smoke dragons again positioned themselves in such a way as to force them to the gate. Jaxson looked at Zero and nodded. As they stepped toward the castle, the gate began to swing inwards slowly. As soon as they were beyond the wall, the smoke dragons dissipated once more. Jaxson and Zero were alone inside the vast courtyard. When the gate closed behind them, a chill ran up Jaxson's neck. They were here now; what that was worth, he had no idea.

CHAPTER 6

From where they had first landed, the castle had appeared to be directly behind the wall. Once they had passed through the gate, Jaxson realized the castle was actually much larger and much farther away. A path lined with evenly spaced elms and oaks before them led directly to one of the seven tall towers. Jaxson looked up to the top of the tower and was amazed to see it was just as large at the top as it was at the base. Beyond the tower loomed the ancient castle.

"I guess we should have a look around?" asked Jaxson.

Zero nodded, and they set off down the path toward the tower.

"*It's strange. These trees are thriving. The grass is green and lush without weed or bramble,*" said Zero.

Jaxson could not see a brown leaf nor vine nor weed in any direction. "That is no more strange than anything else," he replied.

"*Yes and no. That fact alone is not that strange, but couple it with the fact we have not seen another living being of any kind in this valley… and it starts to feel odd. Who is maintaining these grounds? Why have we seen no animals? Not a single bird? Something is just off —*"

Jaxson stopped in his tracks and turned his head to the right. "Do you hear that?"

Zero turned and brought his head lower to be on Jaxson's level, in order to see under the trees. Then he laughed. "*And I see the source!*"

Both sprinted to the sound of running water. A stone, three-tiered fountain below a statue of a dragon flowed with crystal-clear water. After they had filled their bellies to the bursting point, Jaxson stepped back to admire the artistry of the fountain. The pool was oblong and longer than Zero, and it was cut from a single solid stone. The bottom tier of the fountain was midnight black and about half the size of the pool. The middle tier was fire-ash gray stone, flat like the bottom and about half the size. The top stone, from which the water flowed, was solid white. The flying dragon statue in the center of the white stone had a single back claw resting upon it.

"That statue has horns like you," commented Jaxson.

"I am quite certain horns on a dragon are commonplace."

"I don't think so. I've never read about any dragons with horns like yours, and the only dragons we have seen didn't have them either," said Jaxson, looking at Zero's two crescent-shaped horns on the top of his head. The same dark green that covered his back also adorned the horns, which arched toward each other and almost touched at the tips.

"It is of no consequence," replied Zero.

Jaxson opened his mouth to continue the debate, but then a dark shadow blocked out the sun. For a moment, he thought a storm must be rolling in, although they had seen no clouds within the storm of the Bend. A dragon more than twice the size of Zero flew overhead, angling to the first tall tower to which the path led. It was darker than night and seemed to swallow the light around it. It circled the top of the tower and flew back in their direction.

"Let's go!"

Jaxson scrambled onto Zero's back, and before he was set in the harness, Zero sprang from the ground. With three powerful beats of his wings, they were above the giant elm trees. The black dragon quickened its pace and was on top of them in an instant. Zero attempted to veer left but the giant dragon stopped in the air above them and beat his wings to send a powerful gust of wind down. Zero could not withstand the gale. He was forced to retreat to the ground or risk being blown into a tree.

Satisfied, the black dragon circled high and then slowly made his way to the ground near the fountain. Jaxson expected

NOTHING MORE THAN ZERO

the ground to shake when he landed, but he was surprised how gently the black dragon set down. He was massive, long and thick, solid black except a hint of gray along the belly and around the face. He had a pair of crescent-shaped horns atop his head, their tips almost touching just like Zero's. When his gaze fell upon them, Jaxson was bare as though the black dragon saw him completely, right down into his soul. He locked eyes with the ancient dragon and then could not look away.

Finally, the black dragon spoke. *"Is he your rider? Or is he your captor?"*

Zero glanced at Jaxson, then back to the dragon. *"I am not his prisoner, if that is what you are asking."*

"What is your name, young one?"

"Zero is the name I am called. But my hatching name is Zerrophidious. I do not know why I have told you. Only I and he know it."

"It is an old name, a strong name. It suits you." Zero bowed his head as the black dragon continued, *"You may call me Forseti, though that is not my hatching name nor my fire name. Now, what are you doing with this weak one?"*

Until that moment, Jaxson had sat quietly, in awe of Forseti's size and majesty. "What makes you think I'm weak? Because I'm small or because I'm human?"

Forseti turned quickly at the sound of Jaxson's voice. His mouth hung open as he looked from Jaxson to Zero and back again. Then he threw his head back and roared with laughter, long and hard. When he caught his breath, he said, *"Bless the Seven Gates! We have much to discuss."*

CHAPTER 7

The second floor of the castle was open and airy. Every two hundred feet, colossal columns rose from the floor to the ceiling, their tops almost out of sight. Their number was hard to determine. Jaxson could see seven in one row, but he couldn't see the far side of the chamber. They had followed Forseti around to the rear of the structure back and through an open gate larger even than the gate in the outer wall. He led the duo to a fire ring close to one of the columns on the left side of the chamber. Zero settled on the side opposite to the black dragon and watched as Forseti blew dragon's fire onto the rocks within the fire ring. Jaxson shielded his eyes from the blast of heat. When he looked back, a pleasant, albeit large, fire was crackling in the ring.

"Now, we are all settled. I must ask, how did you pass through the Taufan?"

"You mean the storm? I'm not completely sure, but I think we just flew through it." Jaxson glanced at Zero, who gave a slight nod.

"Flew through it? What would cause you to even attempt it?"

"It's not like we had much of a choice. Steam drakes have been hounding us for two days, and then we almost landed on a petridrake," said Jaxson. Each word he spoke came quicker than the last. "We thought we'd lost them when Zero put the petridrake in the others' path. He is hurt; I am exhausted. And still we had to use the storm, the Taufan, to finally escape them!"

Jaxson's chest heaved and sweat beaded his brow. There had not been time to really think about the dangers they had only narrowly escaped. He knew they were lucky to be alive and – more or less – in one piece. The steam drakes had pursued them much farther than was typical of their kind. And the petridrake... he had never seen one before, or even heard of one living in the Dragon Spine Mountains.

"And the sentinels? How did you avoid them to gain access to the gate?"

Jaxson started to reply, but Zero talked over him. *"The smoke dragons? They were on us from the moment we broke free of the clouds. If we stopped, they stopped. If we moved, they guided us. Guided us here."*

"Interesting," replied Forseti. He turned to the column and studied the intricate carvings. There were words, but not of a language Jaxson could read.

"So, what is this place?" asked Jaxson as he moved closer to the column.

Forseti glanced at him but did not answer. Jaxson shuffled his feet and looked around the chamber. The silence stretched on. Zero stared intently at Forseti, then abruptly turned away.

"What's wrong, Zero?"

"This is a strange place, but I am not sure I believe everything he tells me."

"What has he told you? What have you told him?" Jaxson demanded. He moved quickly to Zero's side, never taking his eyes from the black dragon, Forseti.

"I have told him nothing he did not need to hear, though it may be difficult to comprehend," said Forseti. He turned from the column to face them fully. *"Zero insists that I speak with both of you from here on, and I will honor his wishes. You asked what this place is. It is the Temple of Greeti and home to one of the seven portals linking all parts of this world together. I am its guardian and have been for the last age. You are the first outsiders I have spoken to in a very long time."*

"That does not seem hard to believe, given everything we have seen so far," said Jaxson.

"I do not believe that is the part Zero is struggling with," said Forseti, looking at Zero. *"Perhaps he should tell you."*

Zero's eyes widened, and he looked back and forth between Forseti and Jaxson. He took several steps away from Jaxson, shaking his head.

"Zero, it's fine. Tell me what he said that bothers you."

"He told me that he is old – very old. He told me that his time on Kealqua is passing, and that I am..." Zero trailed off and looked at Forseti. *"I won't do it!"*

"Won't do what?" asked Jaxson.

"He says I am to be his replacement as guardian here. It is what I was hatched to do!"

CHAPTER 8

A constant breeze blew through the second floor of the castle overlooking the lush valley. They had entered on the opposite side, and now they were nestled up next to the mountains again. The storm clouds of the Bend – or the Taufan, as Forseti had called it – shifted and spun around, ever changing and yet always the same. This was the first time Jaxson could study the unnatural storm up close, without being in the midst of it or being chased by steam drakes. He found it to be beautiful yet terrifying. Zero had been silent since Forseti had told him of his new responsibility. Jaxson did not understand exactly what it meant, but he knew Zero was completely against it.

"Why are you pouting?" he said.

The green dragon's nostrils flared, and Zero responded, *"I do not pout. I am just thinking."*

"You want to fill me in?" asked Jaxson, watching the Taufan rage on.

Zero was silent for a long time. Finally, he said, *"I am not sure how much to believe. Forseti says he can show me the truth, but I need to be willing to see it. Everything he tells me is cryptic. You know he is old, but not how old. He is ancient, older than the Bend itself. He flew over these mountains before elves arrived, and before men. But none of that matters. What matters is that he claims I am a descendant of an ancient line of dragon kings, for lack of a better word. He is of the same line."*

"That's amazing. He told you all that?"

"Yes and no. He did not speak to me, but something more. He opened up his memories to me – or more accurately, he pushed them

upon me."

"That's amazing! But does that mean we will have to stay here? What would we be protecting? This old castle? It's nice and all, but I'm not sure it needs full-time security. Nobody can get through the Bend." Jaxson began to pace back and forth along the wall overlooking the valley.

Zero watched Jaxson walk in little circles. *"I saw something in the memories... I am not sure if he intended me to or not. It could explain some of it, I think."*

Jaxson stopped pacing and looked at Zero. "Well?"

"I caught only a glimpse before the memory moved on, but I think what I saw was important. It was an archway in the middle of a stone room – big, like everything else here – but I couldn't see through it. It was midnight black, but not solid. It rippled like water with a breeze on it. I could see to either side of it, but within it... nothing."

Jaxson resumed his nervous walking. "And you think this archway is important?"

Zero nodded.

Jaxson continued, "And it's here in the castle?"

"I believe it is." Zero rose to his feet as Forseti glided around from the side of the castle toward the duo. He angled his body slightly and came to a rest just outside of earshot.

"Now we'll get some answers," said Jaxson. "Come on."

As Zero followed Jaxson, he muttered, *"To get answers, we need to know what questions to ask."*

CHAPTER 9

Forseti flew out of the large opening and into the sky guiding them to the uppermost level of the castle. After they landed beside him on the open balcony, Forseti talked about an age before men and elves, about the seven great dragon kings that ruled the world with honor and balance. He told them about the seven portals that linked all of Kealqua together, which were created by the first wizards. He spoke of grand cities which featured places of learning and spirituality. The world had been connected and thriving. Elves came first to the island region of Nebur, then other places. Men followed afterwards, in Specerin and Crystal Vale. The dragons nurtured both infant races, and eventually the dragonriders of vast magical powers came to be. All of this was before the Blank Years.

"What are the Blank Years?" asked Jaxson. "I'm sure I've heard that phrase before, but I don't know what it means."

Forseti gave a deep sigh. *"The Blank Years are not a time forgotten or lost, as the name may suggest. It was a time of no advancement and even serious regression. The study of magic took a dark turn, making some dragons regret ever teaching elves and humans the art. Wars broke out on a scale unseen before. New races that thrived on destruction entered the world. The numbers of orcs and goblins multiplied rapidly. Every aspect of the world the dragon kings had attempted to build took a step backward. It was at the end of the Blank Years, after a terrible war that I will not discuss now, that it was decided by the elders of my race to seal the portals from each other and from the world."*

"You have been here alone all this time?" asked Zero.

"I was not alone at first... but it has been only me for quite some time now," responded Forseti.

"I'm sorry," muttered Jaxson. "My dad left me and Zero a few summers ago, to go and battle the people that would seek to hurt Zero. I know it's not the same, but I miss him terribly."

Dusk came quickly in the valley. The sun had already fallen behind the mountains, and the shadows lengthened rapidly and grew darker. Eerie stillness settled across the valley, and all was still on the top floor of the Temple of Greeti. Jaxson was lost in thoughts about his father, the reason they were in the mountains in the first place. Zero stared out at the coming night, as perfectly still as a statue.

Forseti broke the silence first.

"I settled with my grief long ago. It is still there, a piece of me. But it is rare for it to catch me unprepared. It does happen from time to time, though, and in those moments, I have found it best to allow it to run its full course. Shutting it down within me never did any good. Now, I understand you are not dealing with grief but with uncertainty and fear. But you have already taken the most important step. You are moving forward and not allowing the fear to paralyze you. I commend you for that, Jaxson."

Jaxson nodded, unsure how to respond. Since they had left their little mountain home to search for his father, nothing had gone to plan. He had left with Dreknoxious, an old family friend that Jaxson suspected was something other than he claimed to be. Then the perilous flight through the night, and the next day's attempt to escape the steam drakes and the huge petridrake. They had sought safety in the Bend, and as amazing as this place had turned out to be, now Forseti was telling them Zero had to stay, to be a guardian. They hadn't even left the mountains yet, and everything had gone wrong.

"Forseti, in the vision you showed me, I saw a large doorway filled with darkness," said Zero. *"Was that the portal you spoke of earlier?"*

"It is... and it is the reason you must remain here as guardian of this temple," replied Forseti. *"Let me show you."*

He turned away from the valley and walked into the long, narrow hall. They walked in single file for a time, lacking enough space for both dragons to walk side by side. The hall ended abruptly at a stone wall. Forseti turned his massive head and whispered, *"Believe there is no wall."*

He stepped directly into the wall.

Jaxson's mouth fell open as the black dragon appeared to melt into the stones with each step. When he was gone, Jaxson walked up to the wall and raised his hand to strike it. He expected his hand to pass straight through the stones, but was surprised when his hand smacked the surface, hard. A pained welp escaped his lips, and he waved his hand rapidly.

As Jaxson shook his throbbing hand, Zero laughed.

"What's so funny?"

"You look like a chicken flapping its wing," said Zero.

"Well, it hurts! What are we supposed to do now?"

"We need to believe there is no wall," replied Zero.

He took a deep breath and stepped forward, passing Jaxson and walking through the wall.

"Zero – are you all right?"

"Yes. Just focus on your next step and know *nothing is going to stop you,"* said Zero.

Jaxson took a deep breath. The wall looked and felt solid. When he took a step forward, his head smacked solid stone with a thud.

"Well, that didn't work," said Jaxson as he rubbed the rapidly swelling knot on his head.

"Here," said Zero, and his tail appeared through the wall beside Jaxson. *"Grab my tail. We will do this together."*

Jaxson rested a hand on the tough scales and allowed himself to be pulled through the wall.

CHAPTER 10

"I did not believe you would be able to pass the barrier. You surprise me, and that is not easily accomplished," said Forseti to Jaxson. When Jaxson did not respond, he continued, *"There is more to you and your relationship with Zero than I first thought."*

"What is that supposed to mean?" asked Jaxson.

"All in good time," replied Forseti. *"But first, Zero, you and your rider need to see this."*

Jaxson looked past the ancient dragon, and he saw the doorway Zero had mentioned earlier. It was taller than even Forseti, and easily wide enough for both dragons to pass through side by side. Its frame was made out of a stone that Jaxson did not recognize. It looked smooth and rough at the same time, depending how the light touched it. At the top of the frame were three rubies the size of dragon eggs. The precious stone on the left glowed with inner fire. As interesting as the frame was, the black, rippling surface suspended within it was doubly so. Jaxson couldn't tear his eyes from the shimmering portal. It was pulling at him, wanting him to come closer.

Zero cut between him and the massive doorway as he circled to its rear. Jaxson was finally able to look around at the rest of the room. Although still huge, it was the smallest chamber they had been in thus far. He looked back at the wall through which he had passed, and was surprised to find it was no longer there. Even the hallway was gone. Instead, only a wide-open chamber that ended at the far landing. Zero completed his pass around the doorway and settled beside Jaxson.

"It is a free-standing structure," said Zero. *"The only difference*

is there are no red stones on the back."

"So strange," replied Jaxson.

Forseti circled the doorway, and once behind it, Jaxson could only see a ghostly shadow through the door. When the black dragon returned to the front, he stopped near the glowing red stone.

"It has been an age since one of these stones glowed. The only difference in all that time is that now you two are here," said Forseti. Jaxson started to speak, but Forseti talked over him. *"Now is the time for listening. I will tell you all you need to know. And if you still have questions after I am finished, I will do my best to answer them."*

****

With the history beyond history already explained, Forseti launched into a more personal account of the past. He explained how he and his dragonrider had been chosen to guard the portal as it was sealed away. No one – neither him nor the elders – thought it would be for an extended period of time, much less the thousands of years that had passed. His dragonrider had given up hope long ago and succumbed to his own depression.

Forseti dealt with the passing of his closest friend as best he could. And nothing changed. The Taufan blew around the valley, and no one came to relieve him of his duties. The only change in his routine was when he ventured out of the valley for food, when no roaming elk herds passed through. Even that grew tiresome over the years, when he failed to encounter any other dragons near the Bend.

Still, he fulfilled his responsibility. He guarded the empty portal and the impregnable valley.

Then, fifteen years ago, one of the rubies on the portal began to glow again. Forseti knew that could only mean a dragon of royal descent and his bonded rider were nearby. He had been watching the empty portal as the black, traveling void returned within the archway just yesterday, coinciding with Zero's and Jaxson's entering of the Taufan. But when another ruby did not start to glow, he had lost heart. It was merely a coincidence, or perhaps the magic was failing after so many years. The sentinels had allowed them to pass, however, meaning that Zero, at least, was supposed to be here.

So, these were the reasons Forseti took Zero to be the new guardian of the temple and the portal. He had given up on Jaxson from the first moment, because he did not resemble the dragon-riders of old. He was too young and too scrawny. Forseti had not seen a weapon or a staff. Then Jaxson had passed through the last barrier protecting the portal, surprising Forseti again. Still, the remaining two rubies were dormant. Now, Forseti was unsure if Zero was indeed intended to remain.

CHAPTER 11

The fire crackled as the fat dripped from the elk's hindquarters. Beside the temple, Jaxson rotated the spit quietly under the stars. He drank deeply from his skin he had filled at the well, but it did nothing to sate the hunger in the pit of his stomach. Still, the one thing living alone with Zero in the mountains had taught him was patience. He would not rush it and risk burning the meat – or worse still, his mouth. He would wait for the dragons to return. Zero had flown with Forseti toward the mountains to the north just before sundown, at the older dragon's request. Jaxson had attempted to ask where they were going, but had not received much information in reply.

He took another swig from the waterskin and found it empty. As he strolled through the trees along the path to the well, he tried to decide how he would talk Zero into getting out of here. He needed to find his father, and it was obvious he wasn't here within the Taufan. The original plan, before being chased for a day and night by the steam drakes, had been to travel into the Kingdom of Esther with Dreknoxious in search of any sign of his father. That had all gone wrong. When Forseti had told them that Zero was to be the new guardian, Jaxson's heart had sunk. He would not leave Zero no matter the cost, but he also couldn't abandon his search for his father. He didn't want to admit it, but he was worried about his father. He could think of no reason for him to be away for so long.

He was thinking in circles. He had been worried about his father for a long time, so why was it bothering him so much now? Perhaps he was actually worried about Zero wanting to stay, wanting to connect with his past. Jaxson didn't know the full story of how his father had acquired Zero as an egg. He didn't know any part of the story, really. Although Zero had never asked, Jaxson knew he was curious about his origins. Dragons stay with their young until the little ones are able to fend for themselves, so it was unlikely he was abandoned. Now Forseti had offered a clue to his past, and Jaxson was concerned that the allure would prove too much for Zero to turn down.

He filled his waterskin and decided not to think about it again until he had talked with Zero. He turned to return along the path toward the fire where the mouthwatering meat was cooking.

Jaxson looked left and then right, but there was no path in sight. He walked around the well, thinking that maybe he had gotten himself turned around while deep in thought. On the other side, three paths appeared where he was sure there had been none moments before. The first was wide and smooth, but went to the south, well away from the temple. The middle one was worn but overgrown. It had not been trod by anyone in quite some time. It led directly away from the well – if indeed he was turned around, it should lead him straight back to the temple. The final path was shrouded in shadow more profound than the starlight should cause. Limbs, barren and twisted, from gnarly trees reached over the dark and broken path.

In every fairytale he had ever heard, the easy path was a trap, and only a fool took the most forbidding path. He pondered the middle path that seemed not to have been taken by any for a long while as maybe being his best option. He looked at each path again and took a deep breath. He could smell the grass and the scent of the coming rain, but underneath these was the pleasing aroma of crackling meat over a fire. He focused on the intoxicating scent and turned away from all three paths. He followed his nose all the way back to the fire and the two waiting dragons.

"I told you he would return before daylight," said Zero as he rose to greet Jaxson.

"Well before daylight... which path did you choose?" asked Forseti.

Jaxson looked from one dragon to the other. "Was this some type of test?"

When neither dragon responded, he looked at Zero and asked, "Were you in on it? What was the point?"

"*I wanted to prove—*" Zero began.

Forseti cut him off. "*Which path did you choose?*"

"I didn't take any of the paths. I followed my nose back here!" said Jaxson. "Now what was the point?"

"*You may not have picked one of the three paths, but you did choose,*" said Forseti. "*And again, you surprise me. Zero is right. You are worthy.*"

"Worthy of what?" asked Jaxson.

"*All in due time,*" said Forseti.

"*It is of no concern,*" said Zero. "*We should eat, then sleep. Tomorrow we will be on the path to find your father.*"

Jaxson smiled. Finally, they would be on their way.

CHAPTER 12

The flight back through the Taufan seemed easy compared to their hectic trip only two days earlier. Jaxson hugged Zero's back as he flowed up and down on the strong winds, always moving toward the outside of the Taufan. Forseti had spoken with Zero briefly about not fighting the storm winds to instead use them to his advantage, and it worked. Jaxson did not feel the force in his head threatening to send him back down into the depths of blackness. A full belly and some rest helped.

The sun dazzled him as they broke free from the clouds, low to the ground in between two colossal mountains. The Dragon Spine Mountains ranged to the south and the west. Foothills filled the landscape away to the north, and there was a large forest to the east. There was not a cloud in the sky.

Zero shot straight up into the air, gaining speed as he climbed. Jaxson let out a joyous yell as Zero pulled up and immediately started to plummet back to the rocky ground. Jaxson reveled in exhilarating freedom, his hands in the air and wind blowing through his hair.

There was no need to stick close to the mountains, as the steam drakes had been obliterated on their way into the Taufan of the Bend. Now the pair could go in any direction they wanted – which presented them with a new set of problems. Jaxson knew he needed to go north to the Kingdom of Esther, but he wasn't positive what he would do once he got there. What was more, he knew to go to the Kingdom, but not *where* in the Kingdom. And it was big, stretching from the Dragon Spine Mountains to beyond the Laguza Sea.

However, Zero surprised him, turning to the east to fly alongside the forest.

"Where are we going?" asked Jaxson.

"Forseti told me this forest is called the Heart of Viana, home of the elves," replied Zero. *"We need supplies not available within the Taufan. We can trade for them here."*

"Trade with what? We don't have anything."

"I have a plan, but when we get there, you need to do the talking."

"Why?" asked Jaxson. When Zero gave no answer, he asked again, "Why? What does that mean?"

Zero kept flying, still not answering, so Jaxson settled in and started making a mental inventory of everything they would need. He needed arrows to begin with, and a backup bow string. New clothes wouldn't hurt. He had water, but very little food. Without a pack to carry anything in, the list couldn't be too long.

Still, without anything to trade, making a list seemed pointless. After a time, Zero filled him in on the plan Forseti had given him. Jaxson thought it was a long shot at best.

****

They flew for hours along unchanged forest. The grassy hills to their left were endless. Jaxson spotted a change in the landscape immediately. Two large stone pillars stood just beyond the forest, on level ground where the trees met the hills. A road ran from the pillars onto the rolling plains to the north, where it faded into the horizon.

Zero dropped lower and reduced speed. As they passed the pillars, Jaxson saw nobody. Zero turned slowly and circled back to the pillars once more. The lonely stones did not seem inviting to Jaxson.

The dragon touched down softly on the hillside beyond the pillars. He gestured with his head for Jaxson to approach them. Before he was halfway there, three figures appeared between the pillars. He was sure they hadn't been there moments before, but there was no mistaking the three elves that stood there now. He raised his hand in greeting as he continued to walk forward. The stoic elves, who wore clothes in natural hues of brown, green, and tan, did not respond, waiting as motionless as the pillars beside them. Jaxson continued his approach, still unsure about Zero's plan but beyond the point of backing out. They did need supplies before going into the Kingdom, and before the next leg of their journey to find his father.

"Hello there," he said as he finally came within earshot.

"Greetings from the forest," said the middle elf. "Do you come seeking to trade?"

Jaxson nodded and came to a stop before the elves. The middle elf, the one that had greeted him, was tall and slender, with green clothes and a large eagle feather in his hair. The two on either side were shorter and stouter. One wore tan clothing and wore a small deer antler on a cord around his neck. The final elf wore brown and black clothing and was the only one with his arms exposed. At first, Jaxson thought he saw intricate tattoos from wrist to shoulder, but on closer inspection they appeared to be a second skin fitting snugly in place.

"We are in need of several items, if you have them," said Jaxson.

The elves exchanged glances, and the antler elf said, "You do not appear to come from the north, and therefore you are not one of our regular trading partners. Also, you do not have much to trade, unless your barter remains with your dragon."

"I'll show you mine after you show me yours," said Jaxson.

The middle elf stared at Jaxson, but Jaxson didn't look away. Finally, the elf laughed and gestured for Jaxson to follow as all three of the elves turned and entered the forest.

CHAPTER 13

Once inside the forest, Jaxson noticed there were many more elves than he had expected. Some were traveling along the branches of the trees, and others were busy weaving baskets or tending small gardens. They were lively and spoke with each other quickly but quietly. No one spared him a second glance as he followed the three elves to a circle of rocks around a small fire. He was offered a glass of clear, yellow liquid which he sipped politely. His head danced with visions of spring, flowers and gentle sunlight, and the scents of new grass and the crispness of an early morning frost jolted his senses. The laughter of the elves nearby startled him. Jaxson looked down at the small cup with the clear liquid in amazement.

"First time drinking the drop of the sun?" asked the first elf.

"Yes. It's amazing," said Jaxson. He took a larger mouthful.

"We often forget how the things we find so simple and boring are in fact a wonder to the other races," said the elf. "My name is Grothum, and I will be your trading partner. And your name?"

Something tiny flew directly above Jaxson's head, a blur of green with a spot of red. He tried to follow it with his eyes but couldn't keep up. "Uhh, my name is Jaxson. What was..."

Grothum looked in the direction Jaxson was staring. From the lowest branch of a tall oak, a vine laden with purple flowers cascaded down. Flitting from flower to flower was the tiniest bird imaginable, no bigger than Jaxson's thumb.

"There! What is that thing?"

Grothum laughed again. "It is called a bee bird or, as you humans call it, a hummingbird. Beautiful little creatures that drink the nectar of flowers, and, like bees, help to spread and propagate those same flowers. Have you never seen one?"

"I have not. Most of my life has been high in the mountains. We have fairies but not bee birds," replied Jaxson. "So tiny and its wings are a blur."

"Yes, yes. But perhaps now it is time to get to business," said Grothum.

"You're right, of course. How do we begin?" asked Jaxson.

"Simple. You tell me what you want from the trade. I will tell you if we have it or how long it will take to bring it here," said Grothum. "Then we will discuss what you have to trade for value."

Jaxson looked around but did not see any place to store goods. He didn't think anything would be on hand. "I need some food. Something filling but portable, about five days' worth."

"Have you ever eaten elven food? It is simple fare but, as with that drink, it is all natural. We can provide the food."

"Next, I will need arrows. My quiver will hold about a dozen and a half. And do you have bowstrings? I like to have a backup." Each request was easier for Jaxson to make. If Zero's plan worked and the elves had everything they needed, they would be set for supplies for a good while.

"We can do arrows, and a backup string is always a good idea," commented Grothum.

"Do you happen to have any clothes that would fit me? And shoes?" asked Jaxson.

"The clothing will be no problem as long as you don't mind natural hues? We would normally have plenty of human clothes, but our trading partners to the north traded for nearly all of it last week," said Grothum. Jaxson nodded, and he continued, "The shoes may be more problematic, but I will send a runner to another camp. Perhaps he will be able to acquire suitable footwear for you."

Jaxson listed several other items: a pack, an extra waterskin, and a small knife to replace the one he had lost recently. Grothum did not raise any objection even when the list grew long. He simply sent one elf or another to procure the items. When Jaxson ran out of things to ask for in trade, the runners had already gathered quite a pile behind Grothum.

"Is that all that you require?" asked Grothum.

Jaxson looked at the goods with hopeful glee. Replacement clothes and even shoes sat beside arrows and packages of food. He could not think of a single thing to add, until a flash of feathers zoomed up to the hanging flowers above his head. He said, "One more thing… I would like a feather from one of the bee birds."

Grothum's head flew back in laughter. "What a request! We do not take feathers from our bird friends, but if they are freely given, we carry them. I'll ask one of our tiny friends for you, but do not truly expect any results. Never has one outside of our forest received a feather."

He turned from the fire, and Jaxson heard a low whistle that warbled slowly, then more quickly. As the tune danced, Jaxson imagined one of the small hummingbirds in a sea of flowers, flitting from one to the next, taking in its fill of sweet nectar. Grothum's tune changed, becoming slower and sweeter. A tiny ball of feathers darted down and hovered directly in front of Jaxson's face. Grothum's whistle changed tune again. He extended his hand gently, and the hummingbird lit on his finger. Jaxson saw the long, needle-like beak of the hummingbird bob up and down, and then the bird shook. After the bird flew back to the flowers, a tiny, iridescent feather remained in Grothum's hand.

"This is truly special," said Grothum, almost to himself.

CHAPTER 14

Other elves started to gather around Grothum. He held the feather in his cupped hand, his eyes never leaving it. Jaxson saw the other elves talking quietly but urgently. He saw their furtive glances in his direction, though he never saw anyone looking directly at him. It was plain even to Jaxson, with his limited elven knowledge, that a bird giving a feather in this manner was different and noteworthy. The elf with the full arm sleeves that looked like another skin spoke quietly with Grothum, then approached Jaxson.

"Greetings again. My name is Belhie – we met earlier at the pillars," said the new elf.

"I remember. I thought your sleeves were tattoos at first. They're quite striking," said Jaxson as he studied the diamond shapes that intertwined and flowed up Belhie's arms.

"They are not tattoos, but they are not sleeves either. They are the skin from a mighty tree snake that calls this forest home. He gave them to me many years ago," said Belhie.

"That's amazing! Why did he give them to you?"

"Under normal circumstances, we, the Elves of Viana, would never discuss this with any outsider. These are not normal circumstances, however." Belhie motioned for Grothum to approach, then continued, "This feather was given by one of the bee birds to you. It is an honor, and not one bestowed on anyone outside of the forest of Viana... until now."

"I don't understand," said Jaxson, reaching his hand toward the feather.

"We do not fully comprehend what this means either," replied Grothum. He allowed Jaxson to grasp the feather gently.

A need to make a great journey overcame Jaxson. He knew in his heart it was time to migrate north towards... something. He was thirsty, so very thirsty. A craving for sugar came over him. Slowly, all these urges slid away, and he was once more just Jaxson grasping a tiny feather. He looked at Grothum, then Belhie, with wide eyes. Both elves seemed relieved, and they laughed.

"Quite a rush of emotions, isn't it?" asked Belhie.

"I'm not sure what it was. It was as though I was flying, and then I became thirsty for something sweet. All the while, I had a desire to be moving north," said Jaxson.

"Listen carefully, the bee bird has offered you a feather, and you have accepted. This means you will forever be linked not just to this bee bird, but all of them," said Belhie. His gaze was intense, and Jaxson dropped his eyes. "You must learn to control when you allow the urges and thoughts of the bee bird to enter your mind."

"How is that possible? I was completely overwhelmed by it," said Jaxson.

"The tree snake whose skin I now wear, and the noble one, the eagle, whose feather Grothum has in his hair, are like the bee bird to you. We are linked, and that link is invaluable. If you were an elf, we would guide you on your spiritual journey with the bee bird. Since you are not, we will warn you to guard the feather. When a bee bird is close, the emotions and thoughts of it will be stronger, but you can control how much you it affects you," Belhie told him.

Jaxson wasn't sure why or how this was happening. Even now, he felt the pull to travel north and a thirst for something sweet. "Why did it give me a feather?"

"We may never know," said Grothum. "But I think the primary reason is that you asked."

"And the bee bird sensed something in you. Some sort of kinship," said Belhie.

"Maybe it's because we both desire to go north?" said Jaxson with a shrug of his shoulders.

"It is more than that," responded Belhie. "The bee bird travels north every year only to return later. It goes when its nature pushes it."

Jaxson looked up at the bee birds flitting around the flowery vines. Again, he was almost overcome with their thirst and their desire to move north. He closed his eyes and concentrated on Zero. The strange sensations of the bee birds left him, replaced by the comfortable connection with his dragon. Zero's curiosity about the bee birds was in Jaxson's mind as well as the dragon's impatience to move the trade along. It still wasn't a certainty that his plan was going to work.

"I think I will be able to control it to some degree," said Jaxson. "It's not all that different than when I open up to my dragon."

"That is possible," replied Grothum. "Now, should we discuss what you have to trade for everything else? The feather was freely given, but arrows, clothes, and food have a price."

"We can do that," said Jaxson. "Do you mind if Zero – that's my dragon – joins us?"

CHAPTER 15

Zero walked slowly with his head held high and his wings pushed straight back. He did not look at anyone or anything, but remained the picturesque vision of a dragon. Jaxson was impressed with his friend's stature and bearing. *His plan might work after all,* he thought.

The elves, although they studied Zero scrupulously, did not seem overly impressed. Grothum walked out to greet Zero first. "Welcome, dragon guest. Please, settle by our fire."

Zero looked down at the elf briefly, then passed the fire to stand beside Jaxson. Grothum shrugged and walked back to join the rest of the elves.

Belhie addressed Jaxson. "Your dragon is here, and we have shown you all the requested items in trade. We have provided arrows, clothing, shoes, and even a pack to carry all the food. Now, what do you offer in exchange?"

"Here goes nothing... Are you ready, Zero?" Jaxson said in his mind to Zero. "Well..."

"My name is Zero, Dragon of the Greeti, descendant of the dragon kings of old. I request an audience with the Elven King Rhomius," said Zero.

Jaxson heard him loud and clear, but the elves made no indication they did. His brow furrowed, and he glanced at Zero. The dragon remained stoic, looking straight ahead. All of the elves had stopped chatting or working, the first indication they had heard Zero loud and clear.

Finally, Belhie stepped forward. "You claim to be a Dragon of the Greeti. But I wonder if you even know what that means?"

said the elf loudly. When Zero did not acknowledge him, he continued, "Of course, you would attempt to invoke the name of Greeti when you have nothing to trade for the goods we have provided. And you demand to speak to our great Cyren Rhomius? How bold!"

Jaxson edged nearer to Zero. He wanted to be close in the event that a quick departure became necessary. The other elves laughed at Belhie's outburst. Some said that Zero was no Dragon of the Greeti. He was too small and too young. Even Grothum found it amusing.

All of the elves laughed, except one. He was a tall, slender elf who had only recently arrived and had hovered near the edge of the deep forest. Now he walked up to Zero, chin held high and shoulders back. His fine white hair was braided loosely down his back. His presence silenced the elves.

"Zero, claimant of the title Dragon of the Greeti, can you prove you are what you say?" asked the new elf.

For the first time since making his proclamation, Zero moved. He lowered his head level with the newcomer. They locked eyes for a long moment. Once again, Jaxson became nervous. The plan had been simple. Claim Zero was a Dragon of the Greeti, and when he was asked how he could prove it, he was to say Forseti's name. Zero locking eyes with a powerful elf was not the plan.

The new elf lowered his head and closed his eyes. Zero resumed his stoic stance once more, but his eyes remained on the elf.

Finally, the elf spoke. "This dragon's claim is true. I swear it by the tiny gods and my father's throne. Zero is a Dragon of the Greeti, and the first to enter our forest in thousands of years. Let us rejoice."

The other elves stood with open mouths, staring at the new elf. Then almost as one, they gave a triumphant yell. Grothum threw his arms in the air and danced around. Belhie sank to his knees with tears in his eyes.

Jaxson looked on with utter shock. This was not the reaction he had been expecting.

"Forseti warned me this might happen," said Zero, speaking only to Jaxson.

Quietly, Jaxson responded, "Did he? I didn't realize you two had this all planned out."

"The elves that dwell in this forest, in the Heart of Viana, have ever been allies to the Dragons of the Greeti," said Zero. *"I have just told the tall elf the answer to a question that is thousands of years old. The elves desired to use the portal to return to the other side of Kealqua, but were shut out once the Taufan went up. Forseti is going to allow them to be the first to return to the temple once the Taufan falls."*

The tall elf approached and extended an arm to Jaxson. After a brisk handshake, the elf said, "My name is Calin, Prince of the Heart and heir to its throne. This is truly a special day for us. Anything you need is yours. Zero told me that the two of you will be eager to continue your journey. But know that you are always welcome in the Heart. A Dragon of the Greeti and his rider that was bestowed a feather are always welcome."

CHAPTER 16

The wind blew through Jaxson's hair, forcing it back over his shoulders. He smiled as Zero soared over the rolling plains, with the forest in sight near the horizon. They were backtracking, which would normally bother Jaxson, but after all that had happened the last few days, the sun on his face and a full complement of supplies allowed him to relax. Soon they would see the Taufan of the Bend on their left as they flew into the southern regions of the Kingdom of Esther. One step closer to finding his father.

The encounter with the elves had left Jaxson perplexed. Zero knew more about the Temple of Greeti and the portals than he had let on. When Jaxson asked him about it, Zero said that Forseti had left impressions in his mind the day he had shown him the memories. He knew things now that he had not before. The elves' desire to enter the portal within the temple was one such piece of knowledge, which had circled up to the surface of his mind when its need became obvious. Forseti had sent them to the elves for supplies, understanding that the knowledge within Zero would be of great help.

"What other useful things are you hiding in your head?" asked Jaxson as they flew lazily to the west.

"*I don't know. At least, I won't know until I do… if you understand,*" replied Zero.

"Not really. How did you know about the elves wanting to get to the portal? And the elven king's name?"

The horizon tipped up as Zero banked slowly to remain in the favorable wind. He rarely had to move his wings if the wind held up.

"Did you hear me? How did you—"

"*I heard you. It is not easy to explain. When we first landed and I urged you forward, that was all on the advice of Forseti. When the elves appeared between the pillars, I knew them, and knew them well. But that was impossible. So, I started thinking about all the things I knew about elves. Their desire to return to their homeland through the portal, and their king's name, was simply in my head. I don't really know how to explain it any better than that.*"

Zero leveled out and continued to glide. Jaxson hesitated, then said, "Is everything normal other than these extra memories? Are you well?"

"*Yes, yes. I am fine. Better than fine, actually,*" said Zero. "*I have always wondered where I came from, and now I have an inkling. After we find your father, I intend to find out more. We need to find him.*"

"I agree. I'm just not sure where to start. Dreknoxious was supposed to be with us. He would know," said Jaxson.

They fell into a comfortable silence. Though they weren't sure where Jaxson's father was, Dreknoxious had told them he was in the Kingdom of Esther. The duo was flying in the correct direction, and for now, that was good enough.

****

After passing the Taufan at the Bend, they flew for several hours before finding a likely spot to camp in the foothills below the familiar Dragon Spine Mountains. A small stream bubbled on the far side of the glade, but it was blocked from view by thick undergrowth. Tall trees with long, green needles obscured a view of the mountains behind them. Jaxson started a small fire and snacked on some of the elven food from his pack, and Zero left in pursuit of his own meal. Clouds, lit red and orange, filled the horizon as the sun sank slowly. Night birds were starting to call to each other, and crickets sang their songs to usher in the night.

Jaxson leaned his head back against a large rock and lazily watched the sky for Zero's return. His eyelids were heavy, and he tried to stifle a yawn. He lost that battle and stretched his arms wide. When his mouth closed, so did his eyes.

He awoke to the familiar sounds of wind produced by wings and leaves rustling, as a dragon landed behind him. Without rolling over, he asked, "Did you find enough to eat?"

He could hear Zero move along the edge of the clearing, circling to the fire the long way round. Slowly, Jaxson came fully awake. The stars above and the lack of moon meant he had slept longer than he thought. He sat up. He could hear Zero's low snores as he rested on the other side of the fire.

Then what just landed behind us? thought Jaxson.

A twig snapped behind them. Jaxson whirled around, but the starlight didn't offer much of a view. He strained his eyes and ears, but all he could see was the gentle swaying of the trees against the backdrop of stars and the only thing he could hear was the running water in the creek.

"Zero! Wake up," said Jaxson urgently. He didn't shift his attention from the direction in which he had heard the noise. He backed away slowly until he was beside the fire, and he bumped into Zero's side. He tapped on the rough hide. "Wake up! I think something is out there."

Being this close to the fire ruined what little night vision he had. He made his way to Zero's head, and to his surprise, he saw that the dragon's eyes were wide open and looking in the same direction.

"Do you see anything?" whispered Jaxson.

"Not anymore. I thought I caught a glimpse of a red tail, but it is gone now," replied Zero.

"What is gone now?" boomed a voice in Jaxson's head.

The duo whirled around to find a massive, red dragon standing over them. His head was bent down, and its hot breath blew into Jaxson's face. Before they could make a move, the dragon said, *"I wouldn't leave so soon. It has taken me days to find you!"*

CHAPTER 17

After the initial shock of a giant, red dragon sneaking up on them had worn away, Jaxson found himself relieved to finally have some direction. Tollison had been sent to locate Jaxson and Zero by none other than Dreknoxious. There had been some back and forth concerning how Tollison knew the old man, but Jaxson was satisfied that Tollison's claim was true. Jaxson didn't feel the need to divulge all that he and Zero had seen recently, and Tollison did not ask.

"On your way, and even once you arrive, you need to be on guard," said Tollison.

"For what?" asked Jaxson as he shoveled more of the elven food into his mouth. It was late and, after the scare, he found himself to be starving again.

"Bounty hunters, of course! Did Dreknoxious tell you nothing of what you are flying towards?" responded Tollison with wide eyes.

"The last time we spoke, there were other things to worry about," said Jaxson.

Zero moved away from Jaxson a little, apparently no longer believing Jaxson needed protection. *"So, what are we expected to encounter?"*

"I have no idea! But on your way to Goulage, be on the lookout for bounty hunters. They will travel in small groups of three or four. Most will be armed well and be upon armored mounts. Only occasionally will with they be in the company of a dragon," said Tollison.

"Bounty hunters? Why should they be interested in us?"

Tollison sighed, and the wind from his breath almost tipped Jaxson over. *"You really are ignorant of the world. Riding a dragon is a capital offense in Esther. And of foremost concern, Zero is an unregistered dragon. That will draw attention in itself. You would be wise to be more stealthy when you camp at night, for the remainder of your journey."*

"We hear you. Tell us about Goulage," said Jaxson. Zero and Jaxson listened patiently as Tollison talked at length about the small town of Goulage.

In years past, Goulage had been a bustling town on the verge of becoming a major city. Two major trade routes passed through the town, and the townsfolk spent much of the money made from the three mines with the passing traders. However, with the decline in travelers coming from the south out of Crystal Forge and tensions with the people from the west, fewer and fewer traders came through the town. The mines were mostly bare, and the people were too tired to keep digging. Goulage was a shadow of its former glorious state. Still, Tollison said there were some good people left, although many had "lost their way."

"Aren't dragons common in the Kingdom of Esther?" asked Jaxson.

Even though it was dark, Tollison turned and looked in the direction of Esther. *"Not as common as we once were. I have not been over the plains of Yallwen, as we dragons call it, in many years. I refuse to wear the mark required by the king now."*

"What is the mark?" asked Zero.

"No matter. Meet Dreknoxious in Goulage near the great fountain on the north side of town," said Tollison. *"He will explain anything he thinks you need to know. As for me, I am set to depart. Good tail winds to you."*

Zero bowed his head, and Jaxson waved.

"It was an honor to meet you!" Jaxson said. "I hope our paths will cross again soon."

Tollison chuckled. *"So wonderful to talk to a human other than Dreknoxious. Though I am not sure he is really human. Regardless, you two be careful."*

Tollison left their camp as the sun rose. Jaxson yawned and looked at Zero. Without a word, they both settled down for a nap before starting the trek to Goulage. Jaxson's father would have told him to never go to a strange place tired or hungry.

CHAPTER 18

Jaxson and Zero decided to follow Tollison's advice on a more cautious route for the next few days. They moved back into the mountains that ran almost due west. No fires after dark made their traveling days shorter but safer. They still did not stand watch all night, but did take effort to find sheltered areas to rest. One night they slept in a shallow cave, and the next in a thick stand of evergreen trees near to a ridge. The extra precautions weren't ideal but worth the hassle if they could make it to Goulage unscathed.

Jaxson had to convince Zero it was best for him to go into town alone first, to determine the lay of the land. The dragon found a small cave that overlooked the path from the mountains to the farms on the outskirts of the town. Jaxson figured if he left at daybreak, he would make it into Goulage by midday.

The next morning came quick and bright. As Jaxson made his way down the path, he stayed in constant communication with Zero. They needed to test how far they could be from each other and still communicate. Even when Zero was out of sight, they could hear each other. The farther he went down the path, however, the fainter Zero's voice in his mind became. By the time he had passed through the farms and into the outer edge of the wall-less city, Jaxson could only gauge the dragon's emotions, rather than actual words. He could understand Zero's anxiety and tried to send calming sensations back.

It was difficult for Jaxson to send Zero happy thoughts as he looked at the state of the town. Large ruts lined the roadways. The wooden tiles on the nearby roofs were warped and splintered. Each step he took provided new evidence of slow decay. Weeds littered what had probably once been a spice garden outside one home. Trash filled the alley between two larger buildings. Everything from the buildings to the streets and from the peoples' clothing to the wagons they maneuvered was worn down and neglected. Even his travel-worn clothes were better than the attire of the few residents moping around. They kept an eye on Jaxson without making direct eye contact. Each time he passed a townsperson, the back of his head tingled with their stares.

Worry wormed its way into his head, and Jaxson, out of fear his dragon would overreact, had to send reassuring thoughts back to Zero. As he approached the center of the town, he heard a crowd ahead. He stepped around a corner to enter a large, cobblestoned square. Like everything else in Goulage, it was clear that it had seen better days. Stones were cracked or missing. At the edges of the square were displayed pitiful goods on ragged stalls. But what caught Jaxson's attention fully were the people. Most were on his left-hand side, fewer on his right. The two groups were separated by a single, empty gallows. The wooden frame appeared to have been cobbled together using anything easily obtained, and it seemed to Jaxson that the whole thing might tip over and collapse at any moment. Shouts came from both sides, but the majority drowned out the smaller group.

"Death is justice! Hang him! Death is justice!" the majority chanted.

The smaller group yelled back. "Freedom! Not guilty! Freedom!"

Jaxson concluded that the two groups were one spark away from exploding on each other, and he didn't like the smaller group's chances. *I don't need any part of this,* he thought, and ducked backwards into an alley, still keeping an eye on the crowd behind him. Suddenly, he was flat on his back, struggling against flailing arms and legs on top of him.

"Hey! Wait, slow down," yelled Jaxson as he struggled to rise. The young man that he had plowed into rolled off of him, and was quickly on his feet.

"This way," yelled the man. "Follow me!"

Jaxson was unsure why he did it, but he followed the man into an abandoned warehouse and up the stairs. On the second floor balcony overlooking the large bottom floor, they stopped, their chests heaving. Jaxson put his hands on his knees and followed the man's gaze to the door through which they had entered. When it became clear that no one had followed them, the man turned and stuck out his hand.

"Sorry about that, pal. Name is Tam."

Jaxson shook Tam's hand. "Jaxson. Who were you running from?"

"I wasn't running from anyone," said Tam with a chuckle, but again his eyes scanned the bottom floor.

"Who are you looking for, then?"

"What? No one. I'm just looking," replied Tam.

Jaxson nodded. He pointed behind Tam to the bottom floor. "Then who is that?"

Tam didn't hesitate. He was running again. Jaxson laughed but followed. When Tam stopped, Jaxson said, "Not running from anyone, huh?"

"Well, I guess I wouldn't mind avoiding the sheriff or anyone from the McNair family, for the time being," said Tam.

"Any particular reason?" asked Jaxson.

"Let's just say the spot of trouble Lil' James McNair is in right now might be my fault."

Jaxson shook his head. "I don't know what you're talking about."

Before Tam could reply, a large, muscular man grabbed him from behind. Jaxson turned to flee, only to see three more men dressed in uniforms similar to the first coming up the stairs. Jaxson turned in a circle, then put his hands in the air.

"You look awful spry for a dead man, Tam," said the big man.

Tam smiled and shrugged his shoulders as best he could while being restrained. "I feel pretty good too, Sheriff."

"Let's get you to the old barracks. No way we're going anywhere near those gallows," said the sheriff. He pointed at the men behind Jaxson. "And bring his friend there. If Tam here is dead, no telling what that fella is up to."

CHAPTER 19

Water dripped constantly onto the stone floor of the long-abandoned barracks. The only fixtures in the windowless room were four cots filled with semi-fresh straw, two sconces with burning torches, and one bucket for relief. The solid wood door had a sliding panel which the sheriff pushed aside to check on them from time to time. Jaxson paced while Tam slept. He had tried to plead his case to the sheriff, to tell him he was new in town and had never met Tam before they crashed into each other in the alley. Although the sheriff had seemed to believe the story, Jaxson was still no closer to getting out of the barracks cell.

Jaxson pressed his ear to the door. After a few moments of silence, he crumpled to the ground. His hands cradled his head, and his foot stamped rapidly. He had no idea how or why he was in this temporary jail, but he knew he had to get out.

"Is it all quiet?" asked Tam, one eye peeking through his long, disheveled hair. "Good, I can quit faking now."

As Tam sat up, Jaxson's mouth dropped open. He shook his head without taking his eyes off of Tam. "Why were you faking sleep?"

"Didn't want to answer any questions."

Jaxson snapped to his feet and took a couple of steps toward the lounging man. "Well, you should have kept faking, because I have a few questions myself."

Tam sighed and rolled smoothly into a sitting position. "Guess I owe you that much, friend. Shoot."

"Why did everyone think you were dead?" asked Jaxson.

Tam chuckled to himself then rose to his feet with exaggerated effort. "You get right to it, don't ya? I guess most everyone around here thinks I'm dead cause that's exactly what I wanted them to think."

"Why?"

"I am not sure I need to answer that one," said Tam with a smile.

"Fair enough. What does that have to do with the family you mentioned? The McNairs?"

"You were paying attention," mumbled Tam. "Let's just say the McNairs and my people have never really seen eye to eye. So, when I died, I made it look like one of them did it."

"But you aren't dead," yelled Jaxson as he turned and paced the small room.

"Being dead would put a damper on my ability to keep on having fun," said Tam. He threw his head back and cackled wildly.

"What in the tiny gods' kingdom is wrong with you?"

This only made Tam laugh harder, doubling over with the strain. Jaxson turned to beat once again on the door. His patience with this whole situation had reached its limit. There was no reason for the sheriff to be holding him. One conversation with both of them would prove there was no way Jaxson would be associated with Tam. He beat on the door again but could hear nothing on the other side.

"*What is the problem?*" asked Zero in his head.

Jaxson started. Zero's voice in his head was really weak. Zero must still be a good distance from him. He closed his eyes and thought only of his dragon. "*Nothing. Everything is fine.*"

"*Where are you, then? I have sensed you are nervous,*" persisted Zero.

"*I'm in jail, but it's nothing to do with me,*" replied Jaxson. "*I expect to be out of here soon.*"

"*Jail? Do I need to come get you?*" asked Zero. "*I can be in town in moments.*"

"*No. At least, not yet. What do you mean, you can be here in moments? You're supposed to be in that little cave.*"

"*I am flying above the clouds. No one will see me. And if they do, they will probably think I am a noble one."*

"A noble one! Ha," said Jaxson. "Just stay out of sight."

Tam's eyes narrowed and he leaned closer to Jaxson. "What are you muttering about eagles for?"

"What? Oh, didn't realize I was talking out loud," replied Jaxson. He looked down at his shirt and busied his hands with flattening out the many wrinkles of the elven clothes.

"Maybe... But you were talking with something. Talking with your head," said Tam. "Is it eagles? You can talk to birds?

"You're crazy," said Jaxson, sure he could not trust the young man who had faked his own death for whatever reason.

"I know that look you had," said Tam, standing up. He started pacing. "Personally, I don't like talking with birds. Their minds are so... different. Small animals – now, them I get. Always looking for a meal."

Jaxson stared at Tam for long moments as he worked through what he was saying. "You can talk with animals? You?"

"I can speak with most animals, but rats are the easiest for me," replied Tam.

"No way."

Tam stared at the far wall. It was the first time since he had stopped faking sleep that he had been still. The cell became eerily quiet. Jaxson shuffled his feet, and even that noise seemed muted.

Then a scruffy, long-tailed rat popped out of a tiny crack in the wall. It scurried straight to Tam and hopped on his knee. Tam leaned close and gave the rodent a seed from his pocket. He whispered something to the rat, and it raced back to the crack and disappeared.

"Wow! I don't... I didn't even know people could..." said Jaxson, still staring at the crack in the wall.

"I've just always been able to talk with them. I don't know anyone else that does it. Well, until now," said Tam. The young men locked eyes. Jaxson looked away first, and Tam gave another belly laugh. "Never a dull moment in Goulage!"

CHAPTER 20

The ceiling of the makeshift cell stayed the same no matter how long he stared at it. The water dripped, and Jaxson stared without seeing. Minutes felt like hours, hours like days. Time became insignificant. The only interruption to the doldrums came from Zero, who checked in on several occasions, always insisting it was time to get involved. Jaxson finally had to promise to "scream" at the first sign of trouble, to make him gain altitude. They didn't need anyone seeing a dragon flying over the town.

Tam slept. *Or he is faking again?* thought Jaxson, for at least the tenth time. When the door to their cell banged open, Jaxson nearly hit the roof, but Tam slept on.

Jaxson met the indifferent eyes of the sheriff with a silent plea. He wanted to get out of here. He *needed* to get out of here. He had done nothing wrong, and still he was in the cell. So, when the sheriff spoke, Jaxson clung to every word, eager to please.

"You don't know Tam?" asked the sheriff. When Jaxson shook his head indicating he certainly did not know Tam, the sheriff continued. "So, what are you doing in Goulage?"

"I am just looking for a friend, sir. His name is Dreknoxious, and he is old with a long beard. A really long—"

The sheriff held up his hands, stopping Jaxson short. "No one by that name is in this town. Nor have I ever heard of such a man."

Jaxson's shoulders slumped, and his head hung low. He had hoped that Dreknoxious had been waiting on him, and perhaps had left word with the sheriff about where he could be found. It was a ridiculous thought, a crazy hope, but the time spent staring at the ceiling had put many strange thoughts in Jaxson's head.

"We were traveling together and became separated. But I'm meant to meet him here, I'm sure of it," pleaded Jaxson.

"This place is more dangerous than a drake's nest with fresh hatchlings. I expect you to be moving on, and moving on soon," replied the sheriff, crossing his arms. Jaxson concluded that no amount of reasoning or pleading would affect the man.

"I imagine I will," he replied weakly.

"Stay put for a moment, and I'll get you on your way," said the sheriff. He nudged Tam with his boot. "Come on, boy. There are several people that need to see you still breathing... for the time being."

The sheriff exited the cell with Tam in tow. Immediately, Jaxson heard raised voices. Even though the door was cracked, he couldn't make out exactly what was said. There were multiple new voices, and the conversation quickly became heated. A shrill voice cut over the rest, demanding that "something be done about this nuisance." A loud cackle followed, and Jaxson smiled despite the circumstances. Tam did seem to enjoy the craziness he created.

The voices in the other room dwindled, and then Jaxson heard a door bang closed several times.

The sheriff returned with a scowl. "I'm gonna be straight with you. You need to be very careful getting out of here right now. Like it or not, you were seen with Tam when we brought you over, and that boy has set this whole town against itself."

"I'll be fine, sir. Just let me have my bow and be on my way," replied Jaxson.

"I will, and I'll guarantee your safety to the main road north of town," said the sheriff.

"Thank you—"

The sheriff spoke over him. "If you take Tam with you wherever you're going."

Jaxson cocked his head to one side and looked at the sheriff. He thought for a moment, then asked, "Why would I want to do that?"

"Look, Tam is a good kid, but trouble follows him. Truth be

told, he's the start of most of it. But he's my nephew, and if he stays here, he's a dead man."

"That still doesn't concern me," said Jaxson. He didn't need anything that would slow him down or cause a distraction. If he couldn't locate Dreknoxious, he would go to the capital of the Kingdom of Esther. His search had to start somewhere.

"You're right, of course, but I believe Tam ran into you in that alley for a reason. I don't have a clue what that might be. I just don't think that it's something you should abandon."

Jaxson sighed. He had no reason to take on the burden of a troublesome traveling companion, but perhaps Tam could be useful. His talent with animals could help Jaxson figure out how to use the hummingbird feather effectively. And besides, he didn't want to see the jovial Tam get hurt.

"When do we leave?"

****

Sticking to back alleys and cutting through abandoned buildings, the sheriff led them to the outskirts of the town in short order. The road to the north wasn't surrounded by farms; instead, a thick forest choked out the sunlight. Jaxson told Zero they were moving north and to stay out of sight for the time being.

They had been walking for less than an hour when Tam asked, "Why don't you carry a blade?"

Jaxson glanced at the short sword at Tam's hip and replied, "Never needed one. They aren't very good for hunting."

"There are dangers on the road besides animals," replied Tam. He attempted to pull out his sword, but it stuck in the sheath. He pulled harder, and the blade popped free. Tam reeled and fell into the ditch beside the road.

"Looks like that sword is more dangerous to you than anyone else," snickered Jaxson.

Tam brushed himself off and put the sword away. "I still think you should have a sword, or at least a big knife. Where we going, anyway?"

"I'm headed north to the capital—"

"You have people meeting you out here?" asked Tam. He grabbed Jaxson's arm, bringing them to a stop.

Jaxson peered ahead. "No. Why?"

"My furry friends tell me three fellas are hiding in the bushes just ahead," said Tam.

As the words left his mouth, the bounty hunters stepped forward out of the brush with swords drawn.

CHAPTER 21

Jaxson put his hands out and backed away slowly. Tam pulled out his sword again and kept pace with him.

"We need to get out of here," said Tam.

The bounty hunters laughed. All three appeared to be veterans of many fights, with scars visible on their arms and faces. The two on either side of the tall, bald-headed bounty hunter were shorter, with long, greasy hair. One was missing teeth, and the other had an open wound on his arm that was festering. The only things that didn't look beat up and misused were their weapons. The swords were all clean and straight. There was no filigree or embellishment, just quality, serviceable weapons.

The leader said, "Don't go running off just yet."

"What do you want?" asked Jaxson. Tam had stopped backing away and was a step in front of him. The bounty hunters had stopped as well.

"See, we've been in that little hellhole for quite a while," said the bald hunter. "We know everybody and all the little secrets. It's good to see Tam raised from the dead!"

The bounty hunters all laughed again, and Tam's cheeks reddened. Jaxson slowly slid his hand near to his quiver.

"What does that have to do with me?"

"We've been seeing this dragon circling high above town – trying to go unnoticed, I'm sure," said the hunter. "The only thing I know of that keeps a dragon near this many people is either her eggs have been taken, or its rider is there. No one has any eggs... woulda heard about that. And you're the only new fella in town."

The two men on either side started to slowly encircle them.

C. H. SMITH

The leader continued, "So, we're just gonna take you to the regiment over that way. They pay good money for a rider there."

"If I am a rider with a dragon, how are you lot going to deal with it?" asked Jaxson.

"We'll be gone with you before the flying lizard even knows," said the hunter. "Tam, you should get lost. This don't concern you."

Tam adjusted his grip on his sword but made no move to leave.

"Well then, grab them both."

Jaxson fumbled with an arrow but couldn't get it nocked before one of the long-haired bounty hunters was within sword range. Tam sidestepped in front of him and made an awkward block. His sword hit the dirt road with a puff of dust. Instead of pressing their advantage, the bounty hunters stepped back to laugh at Tam and Jaxson again.

"Boy, you should have run while you still had the chance," the leader said as he stepped forward.

Without waiting for them to remount their attack, Jaxson pulled back on the bow string and loosed his arrow that he had finally seated. A loud *thunk* sounded, followed by the agonizing scream of the leader. The other two bounty hunters wasted no time and charged once more. Before they closed the distance, three large deer crashed into them from the side.

"We need to go, now!" yelled Tam. He pulled Jaxson by the arm into the underbrush, away from the road and the bounty hunters.

"What were those stags doing?" asked Jaxson in between breaths. The boys were moving quickly but Jaxson knew the bounty hunters would be on their trail quickly.

"I told the deer that the bounty hunters were trying to hurt a fawn," said Tam. "They didn't like that."

They stopped to rest and listen for pursuit. Tam had sheathed his sword and stood with both hands on top of his head, breathing hard. Jaxson leaned against a tree and closed his eyes. He let Zero know they were fleeing to the east, and that he thought they had lost the bounty hunters.

Before Zero responded, an arrow struck the tree inches from Jaxson's face.

"Zero, we could use some help!"

"Already on the way."

"We need to find a clearing!" said Jaxson.

"What? No. We need to get into the bush and try to circle back to town," replied Tam.

"Trust me. We need the space."

Tam looked at Jaxson for a moment, then said, "This way. It's a fair piece, so don't dawdle!"

Jaxson stayed on Tam's heels as they pushed through the thick bushes. Brambles and thorns ripped at their clothes, but they kept moving. Jaxson looked over his shoulder for signs of pursuit, and wasn't looking where he was running when a large root tripped him. He sprawled face first just inside an open space in the thick forest littered with old rock. *Ruins of some kind*, thought Jaxson

Tam urged him to the largest rocks at the center of the clearing.

"Well," he said through labored breaths. "Now what?"

"You'll see," Jaxson said simply.

A few minutes passed before he saw movement in the trees near where they had entered the ruins. The leader of the bounty hunters, his shoulder hastily bandaged, emerged from the forest, obviously tracking them. Moments later, the other two appeared on either side.

"Nice try! Now come on out," said the bounty hunter.

Jaxson closed his eyes and stood with his hands raised. Tam pulled at his shirt in a fruitless effort to get him back behind the large rock.

"You caught us," said Jaxson. "I don't want to run anymore."

"I should let Mac put an arrow through your shoulder to even the sc—"

The bounty hunter never finished the threat. Zero landed hard directly on top of him, then spun immediately and slashed with a razor-sharp claw at the bounty hunter holding the bow. The bowman took two staggered steps before collapsing. He did not rise again. The final hunter didn't need any further reason to hit the trees running.

Tam stood up and gaped as Zero walked over.

"Tam, meet my friend."

CHAPTER 22

Jaxson sat laughing at Tam's inability to rationalize Zero's appearance in the glade. Tam watched Zero lounge near the tree line, as far from the bounty hunters' bodies as possible. He started to ask a question for the fifth time, but it sputtered out, again.

"How... Is he *your* dragon?" Tam finally managed.

"Not really mine. More like a really good friend – a brother, really. We grew up together." Jaxson smiled and motioned to Zero. "A really big brother."

"Your *brother*... Is he dangerous?"

"Not to you," replied Jaxson.

Abruptly, Tam bolted to his feet. He paced around for a bit, then muttered something about checking- the bounty hunters. Jaxson had no clue what he was checking them for, but he was glad Tam seemed to have finally snapped out of his daze.

Tam rolled the leader over and searched his vest, then his pants. Jaxson saw him pocket whatever he had found, grab the sword, and move on to the next bounty hunter where he repeated the process. He was quick and thorough. Then he stood and looked around. He walked to where the third bounty hunter had escaped into the woods.

"Where is the third? He should be right here," Tam said, indicating where he was standing.

Jaxson shrugged and then pointed to the trees. "I think he ran that way, screaming in terror. We don't have to worry about him anymore."

Tam ran to the tree line. He threw his hands in the air and kicked at a clump of dirt. "You let him go? YOU LET HIM GO?"

Zero raised his head, and Jaxson held up his hands. "It's fine. He's long gone."

"That's precisely the problem. He'll be back, and he'll have friends with him!" yelled Tam.

"No way he's coming back, not with Zero right there," said Jaxson.

Tam shook his head and muttered to himself. He took a couple steps into the trees, then turned and looked at Zero, then back to Jaxson. "You know, some bounty hunters have dragons too..."

This took Jaxson by surprise. Why would a dragon work with a bounty hunter to track down dragons and their riders? He couldn't fathom it.

"I had no idea," he said doubtfully.

"Really! We need to get out of here. You and your dragon go that way," Tam said, pointing north, "and I'll circle around and go back to the mountains. No way I can keep up with you two."

"Calm down," said Jaxson. "We're not leaving you."

"*I can carry both of you, but not for very far. Back into the mountains is the closest shelter,*" said Zero in Jaxson's head.

"*That's the wrong way, but I don't have a better plan,*" replied Jaxson.

Tam shook his head when Jaxson suggested they both ride Zero into the mountains. After some convincing talk and Zero nudging him playfully, Tam finally relented. Just before Zero launched them into the air, Tam said, "After we find a place to hide out, I can sneak back into town and grab some things. Maybe even *procure* a couple of horses. The sheriff really should've given us some anyway, so it's his fault."

Jaxson let out a yell, happy to be free of the town, free of the jail cell, and on Zero's back in the sky. Tam said nothing else until well after Zero had landed outside a cave that looked livable, at least.

****

The sun was quickly escaping to the horizon when Jaxson, Zero, and Tam entered their newly-found hideout cave. Just inside and lining both sides stood tall pillars of glowing glass. Jaxson stared at the different colors as they danced up and down the flowing glass. He was reminded of a campfire flickering, jumping, possessing a life all its own.

"What is this?" asked Jaxson as he reached out to touch one of the glass pillars. His hand recoiled quickly, then he laughed softly. "It's cool. I expected it to be burning hot... warm at least."

He could see a distorted picture of Tam through the semi-transparent glass as the young man slowly walked around it. Tam, too, reached out to brush his fingers against a pillar.

"Amazing," he muttered. "Never in my wildest dreams..."

"What? Do you know what they are?" asked Jaxson.

The pillars pulsed and flickered, creating colorful light within the cave, which was larger than Jaxson had assumed. Zero was ahead of Jaxson and Tam, but he turned to listen for Tam's reply.

"They must be dragon glass, but I've only ever seen shards and tiny pieces," said Tam. "Even those are very valuable. These must be worth a king's ransom. A dragon first, and then dragon glass unlike any I've ever imagined. What will I see next?"

"I don't know. But we could stay here, or explore a bit," replied Jaxson.

With the dragon glass lighting the way, there was no need for a torch. Jaxson started moving deeper in the cave. Tam sighed, but followed.

CHAPTER 23

The cave widened as they moved slowly deeper into the mountain. The pillars of dragon glass became taller but more spread out, though their burning light still more than sufficed for Jaxson to see where he was going. Zero led the way, keeping a steady pace.

"Ask Tam what he knows about dragon glass," said Zero.

"You seem to know a bit about the pillars. Can you tell us?"

Tam shrugged. "I know the same as everyone else, I suppose. Let's see... Dragon glass glows for a long time – lifetimes, even. And, of course, it's very valuable. I can't even imagine how much all this is worth. I guess several castles, maybe even a whole kingdom. More. I really don't know."

Jaxson stopped and stared at Tam. "That much, really?"

Tam nodded and gestured at the nearby pillars. "I can't even figure it, really, it's that much. Some people say sorcerers and witches seek it for their spells and such. I've never encountered one looking for dragon glass, but that's what people say. And..."

"Go on," Jaxson encouraged him.

"Most people, myself included, believe that it's made by dragons, which is why it is called dragon glass," said Tam. He looked at his feet and turned away from Jaxson slightly.

"You should tell him," Zero said to Jaxson.

Jaxson made eye contact with his dragon, then gave a slight nod in agreement. "My dad told me about dragon glass once, years ago. He said he had held a piece the size of a melon while trading in the Jasmine Sea. He said as amazing as the green, glowing glass was to see, more amazing still was the fact he could *feel* the dragon that had created it. Feel it within him... I wish I'd asked him what he meant."

Tam gave a low whistle. "Well, I don't kn—"

Zero stopped suddenly and lowered his head, peering into the darkness ahead. *"Something is not right."*

Jaxson nocked an arrow and inched forward.

In front of Zero, several pillars had been toppled, and there were shards and chunks of dragon glass littered about. Glass crunched under Zero's massive claws, and Jaxson slipped more than once. There was a bend in the cave ahead, and Jaxson motioned for Tam to stay quiet. Zero extended his neck as far as possible to peer around the corner. Before he could report what he had seen, Tam tumbled to the ground and let out a yell of pain.

"What's happened?" asked Jaxson as he helped Tam to his feet. Zero didn't turn back to watch the commotion, focused instead on what lay ahead.

"Slipped on the glass," said Tam as he brushed himself off. A large blood stain grew rapidly on the sleeve of his shirt.

"How bad is it?" asked Jaxson.

Tam rolled up his sleeve to reveal a long, deep gash running from the back of his wrist clear to the elbow. Blood poured out even as Tam attempted to squeeze the wound closed. Jaxson called Zero over and positioned himself on Tam's opposite side. Before Tam could even ask what they were doing, Jaxson grabbed his wrist gently but firmly. He closed his eyes and focused on the wound. The warm blood oozed out of the cleanly cut skin and lacerated muscle beneath. His breathing slowed and then a tickling sensation began at the back of his mind. He focused on that and sent it through Tam to Zero. Moments later, the sensation returned through Tam's arm, back to him.

Tam watched in awe as the laceration healed rapidly until it was just a thin, aggravated line. The puffy redness around the wound slowly receded until a ghostly scar was all that remained.

Jaxson hung his head and drew ragged breaths.

"Wow. That is amazing," said Tam.

Jaxson struggled to his feet. "It'll be tender for a few days, but other than that, the wound is healed."

"Thank you. Even though I'm not real sure what just happened... thank you."

"You need to rest," said Zero.

"Not here. Do you think it's safe ahead?" Jaxson replied, speaking only to Zero. The dragon nodded his large, green head, so Jaxson said aloud, "Let's get around this bend. I need to find somewhere to rest."

****

As soon as they cleared the corner, the smell hit Jaxson. His head spun, and his stomach threatened to spill its contents onto the cave floor. The odor reminded him of the time his dad had brought home two large turtle eggs in a sealed case. The case had been designed to protect the eggs in transit, and his father was delivering them from a rich merchant to a client. When he had opened the case to show Jaxson the rare eggs, the putrid, rotting stench had struck him in the face. The eggs had been broken for quite some time without his dad's knowledge.

This smell was similar, but far stronger. Tam lost the battle with his stomach and retched loudly. Zero, the only one seemingly unaffected, kept moving forward.

"Jaxson, stay back there. You don't need to see this."

"See what?" said Jaxson, stumbling towards Zero.

He instantly regretted his choice. In a nest of smooth rocks and rounded dragon glass sat two large, broken dragon eggs. Both must have been very close to hatching, because the decomposing remains of the two tiny dragons were hanging out of the shells.

Jaxson turned and barreled back along the cave. He passed the broken pillars and through the beautiful glow without seeing either. He didn't stop until he had passed through the opening and stood under the stars. A light breeze of fresh air hit his face, and he felt better. Then his mind went back to the broken shells and tiny dragon bodies, and he, too, lost the battle with his stomach.

"I told you not to look," said Zero as he and Tam exited the cave.

"I didn't think... What happened to them?"

"Nothing natural. I wonder where their mother is right now."

"I don't know. But I'm sure we don't want to be here if she comes back to find her eggs broken," said Jaxson.

"Are you talking about the mother dragon?" asked Tam. "She has to be long gone. Those eggs have been busted for quite some time."

"You're probably right," said Jaxson. "And besides, I'm in no condition to try traversing these mountains at night. Zero probably shouldn't try to carry both of us either."

"We'll camp right here, then," said Tam. He started to set up a meager camp.

Jaxson just spread out a blanket and fell down on it. The last thing he remembered was Zero taking off to "scout the area," and Tam attempting to spark a tiny bundle of twigs, before darkness overwhelmed him.

CHAPTER 24

Jaxson was last to wake. Tam tended a small pot over an even smaller fire. Zero stood near the edge of the ridge, looking out over the foothills toward Goulage. Jaxson's head still hurt, though the intense pounding of the day before had lessened to a dull ache.

He sat up, and regretted it instantly. After a couple of deep breaths and with immense effort, he made it to his feet. Zero turned to look at him, then resumed his watch. Jaxson walked gingerly over to the fire and sat slowly on the ground. Tam smiled and offered him a waterskin. The water was warm but satisfying. He accepted a bowl filled with a runny stew. Each bite of the stew and sip of the water made Jaxson feel a little more like himself. His head cleared enough to replay yesterday's events.

"Let me get this straight... Yesterday we were in jail, released, attacked by bounty hunters, fled to find a fortune of dragon glass, and finally discovered busted dragon eggs?" asked Jaxson.

Tam kept eating his stew. He nodded. "'Bout sums it up."

"What a day," said Jaxson.

Tam placed his bowl to one side, and looked Jaxson in the eye. "I don't know what to think. I'd never met a dragon before yesterday, and then all this glass..."

He pulled out a handful of the dragon glass shards and chunks. Even in the sunlight, their fiery glow of green, blue, orange, and red was visible. Both young men stared at the glass.

"Can you ask your dragon why they make it?" asked Tam.

Jaxson looked at Zero and tilted his head. "He says he doesn't know, but he had a brief connection with the dragons that made the pillars inside which doesn't seem possible. Some were very old and some newer."

A soft, shuffling sound came from the cave. Jaxson scrambled over to his bedroll to find his bow. Zero flared his wings and moved closer to the mouth of the cave as Tam pulled his short sword.

The group waited quietly, then the sound came again. Jaxson nocked an arrow and drew back the string. He could see movement deeper in the cave.

"Ho there! Don't shoot!" came a familiar voice from farther within the cave. A long, grey beard attached to a frail, old man came shuffling out of the cave. His gnarled staff clicked on the stone and his feet made soft scraping sounds with each step. "I said don't shoot. I am of no threat to you, Jaxson Alpine."

"Dreknoxious? What are you doing here, old man?" said Jaxson with a laugh as he put his arrow back in its quiver.

"Looking for you, of course," replied Dreknoxious.

Jaxson grinned from ear to ear, and even Zero seemed relieved that it was the old man and not something more sinister emerging from the cave. Tam, on the other hand, did not sheath his sword immediately. Instead, he circled behind Jaxson to put as much space between himself and the newcomer as possible.

"Tiny gods! You found me," said Jaxson. "Though I have no idea how."

"The how is quite simple," said Dreknoxious. "We were set to meet in town, and when you did not show, I began searching. I was fortuitous enough to see Zero descending into the mountains late yesterday evening. It has taken me quite some time to locate exactly where, but here you are at last."

Jaxson thought he could detect a smile through the long beard and returned it eagerly.

"Here we are, for sure," he replied. He studied the old man who had visited his father so often in their secluded mountain home. He looked the same as always: old but vibrant wearing his flowing robe with his wooden staff, the same. Then Jaxson frowned. "Dreknoxious, how did you get in the cave without us seeing you?"

"My boy, there is more than one way into the caves of the Dragon Spine. In fact, most are connected," said Dreknoxious. "Now, is there any of that delicious-smelling stew left? I'm starving."

CHAPTER 25

After Dreknoxious had polished off the remaining stew and chewed on a hard piece of bread produced from inside his flowing robes, proper introductions were made. He asked many questions about where Jaxson had been and what had kept him from their rendezvous for so long. Jaxson avoided talking about entering the Taufan at the Bend, or their meeting with the ancient dragon there. He wasn't sure he was ready to reveal those things to Dreknoxious, and definitely not to Tam, who was almost a stranger. Once he had answered all the old man's questions, he had a few of his own.

"You left us abruptly back on the other side of the Dragon Spine Mountains. Did you ever make it back to the group? I was chased off by a whole mess of steam drakes, so I'm not sure what happened."

Dreknoxious's shoulders sagged, and he let out a long sigh. "Bad business. It did not end well, but I am glad you are safe. I was worried."

"And how do you know a dragon?" Jaxson asked, aware that he was peppering the old man with questions. "Tollison is the one that set us on the path to Goulage."

A hearty laugh rose from the old man, and he said, "I have known Ol' Tolly since he was fresh from the shell. There is no one in all of Kealqua I trust more than that overgrown lizard."

"I can't decide if I want to call him Ol' Tolly or an overgrown lizard the next time we see him," said Zero to Jaxson.

Jaxson chuckled. "I don't think I'd call him an overgrown lizard. He doesn't seem like a dragon I would want to offend."

"Perhaps not, but I am too old to worry about such things. I have plenty of other things to keep my mind spinning," said Dreknoxious.

"Like what?" asked Jaxson.

Tam had settled down and watched the two old friends banter. Now he seemed to look uncomfortably out of place. He started to rise, but Jaxson put a hand on his shoulder.

"If you're sticking with me for a bit, you might as well hear what he has to say. I think it's going to be about where we're headed next."

"Right you are," said the old man. "I have begun to fear for Alan, your father. It is not like him to be out of contact with me for this long, but especially not with you. The good news is that I have confirmed his last known whereabouts to be the capital of the Kingdom of Esther."

Jaxson sighed. The capital, bustling with the chaos of a large city, was nothing like he had ever experienced, having spent most of his life in the mountains and trading in small villages nearby. He worried that he wouldn't be able to locate his dad in such a mass of humanity.

"At least we know where we're going," he concluded.

"Yes. You have a destination, but I must warn you. Things are not at all good in Esther, and even worse in the capital," stated Dreknoxious. "The Demon Lizard Death Cult is growing rapidly and is no longer hiding in the shadows. I fear their leaders have the ear of the King, and they are probably why all the bounty hunters are targeting dragons and their riders."

"But some of the bounty hunters ride dragons," said Tam quietly.

"They do, and I don't claim to know how they have convinced the dragons to join their cause. Even the DLDC has dragons, and its purpose is to eliminate dragons from the world of men," said Dreknoxious. "But that is not your only concern. Getting to the capital will itself be a challenge. Goblins are no longer keeping themselves to the mountains. Reports have indicated they have roamed as far as the Triplets to the north. And, of course, you have to evade the bounty hunters, bandits, and even the King's men if you wish to arrive at the capital intact."

Zero lifted his head and peered down the mountainside. Jaxson asked him what was amiss.

Zero told him it was nothing. *"Ask him if he knows what befell the dragon eggs inside the cave."*

"Zero wants to know if you have any idea what happened to the eggs in there," Jaxson said.

"The DLDC and their bounty hunters – that is my first thought," replied Dreknoxious. "Where the mother dragon is, I have no idea. I am going to seal the cave before I leave so whoever committed this foul deed cannot profit from the dragon glass."

"Seal it? How?" asked Jaxson.

"Block the entrance with stones or something. Never you mind that, boy. You should be thinking about how you are going to get to the capital," replied Dreknoxious.

"Which way do you think we should go?"

"I have given some thought to the route you should take. Despite goblin activity near the Triplets, I think you should head to those isolated peaks and then descend to the capital from the west. Zero is less likely to attract attention out there, and perhaps you can come up with a way for him to enter the capital with you," said Dreknoxious. "I assume you have a healthy education in the geography of the region? Yes, I knew your father would insist upon it."

"And once we're there…"

"I will meet you in the gardens of the palace. Check there each morning as the sun rises," said Dreknoxious. Before Jaxson could protest, he held up his hands and continued, "I know I am always leaving, but there is much that requires my attention. My business, which is not your concern I might add, is vibrant and ever changing. If I am as late to arrive to the capital as you were to Goulage, meet with my friend at the castle."

"Who is this friend, and how will I make contact?" asked Jaxson.

"The gardens surrounding the castle are a good place to

start. Ask any of the gardeners where the yellow moon flowers are located. My contact will find you soon after."

Once again, Zero raised his head to peer down the mountainside. A tree branch snapped, and Dreknoxious pushed Jaxson toward the cave.

"Everyone behind me!" the old man screamed.

"What is it?" asked a nervous Jaxson.

"Could be goblins or a petridrake. Or it could be the bounty hunters have tracked you all the way here."

A large stag bounded up the mountain toward the group. It was lathered, and one of its antlers had been torn away. Three wolves broke from the trees in hot pursuit.

Tam rushed to the edge of their camp and closed his eyes. All three wolves stopped and looked at him. He pointed behind him and then back to the trees. The wolves turned and escaped into the forest, leaving their meal to bound away without further harm.

Tam turned and saw that Dreknoxious's mouth was open. "The wolves think there are four full grown dragons up here."

"You are a Ottewn? These are strange times indeed. A human that speaks with animals..." Dreknoxious's words trailed away and he began pacing up and down. Finally, he said, "Jaxson, that is all you need to know. Go find Alan – I fear he may need our help. Tam, I think you would do well to accompany him. I have so many questions for you, but that will have to wait. I must be on my way. Much to do."

Without waiting another moment, Dreknoxious turned and walked into the cave. As he passed, Jaxson thought he could hear him muttering.

Then Dreknoxious shouted, "Step back, boys!"

Jaxson and Tam moved to the edge of the camp, along with Zero, as a large stone fell down the mountainside, coming to rest directly in front of the cave mouth. After the dust had settled, Jaxson could see no way into the cave at all.

CHAPTER 26

The wind carried a chill even this high up Mount Fornessor, the largest in a group of three peaks known as the Triplets. The other two were Fillen and Mijon, both smaller and more rugged than their older counterpart. It was said by the people of the Kingdom of Esther that Fornessor was home to the very first dragon. As the two smaller peaks rose from the land, Fornessor had paid the price. A large crack rose up each side of the older mountain, coinciding with the climb of the smaller peaks. It was the smoothest of the three aside from the cracks and had the most trees. Several small springs flowed down its sides connecting at the base to form a creek that fed into the larger Rillorium River to the east.

Fish and game were plentiful, and the last of the blackberries clung to their vines in defiance of the upcoming winter. The mountain also provided excellent views of the surrounding landscape. The Laguza Sea, which was not really a sea but rather a large lake, was visible to the north. To the west, the lands of the Dahazak stretched well beyond the horizon. Finally, to the east, only an hour's ride by horse and less than half that by dragon, stood the Folja, capital to the Kingdom of Esther. Jaxson stood beside Zero, gazing towards the capital, thinking about all it had taken to get here.

Weeks earlier, Jaxson and Tam had been riding their horses that Tam had procured, heading north along an ill-maintained road. Zero had warned of something unusual ahead, so they slowed. Jaxson nocked an arrow, and Tam pulled out his short sword. What they found though, was carnage. The exact number of bodies was hard to quantify with bits and limbs strewn about.

Fifteen to twenty of the King's men and bounty hunters, littered the road and a small clearing beyond a ditch – all slain. As Jaxson and Tam moved through the field of death, Jaxson spotted the large body of an icy blue dragon, just past the clearing. It was obvious that a great struggle had occurred, but Jaxson couldn't see any bodies of the opposing force. Either they had carried their dead away, or they had come through the battle unscathed.

The young men soon discovered that nothing useful had been left behind. All the bodies had been pillaged. Jaxson studied the dragon's body as Zero landed behind him.

"*What do you think happened?*" he asked Zero.

"*A battle, but against what foe, I cannot say. And what killed the dragon?*"

"I have no idea. Let's go find out," Jaxson responded. Then he said out loud, "Tam, you want to have a look?"

On the armor of the harness attached to the dragon's lifeless body they found an engraved sigil. It was the same as the brand seared into the captured dragons they had seen – and it was Zero's ticket into the city.

From their current camp on Mount Fornessor, it was only an hour's ride by horse and less than half of that upon Zero. Though Folja had seemed so foreign and intimidating on the start of their journey from Goulage, days after finding the dragon's sigil they had encountered an inviting group of traveling traders who had eased some of Jaxson's fears.

Jaxson had seen them first, just off the road before dusk, their wagons circled around a roaring fire. He glanced at Tam, and both angled their horses to the pleasant smell wafting their way. After brief conversation with a foul-smelling guard, Jaxson and Tam were escorted to the fire circle and introduced to a larger-than-life man named Bruton who wore lavish clothing, gold chains, and rings, and who talked loud and laughed louder. It was from him that after several days the duo gained useful information about Folja. But that was after they had made a trade or two.

CHAPTER 27

"First and foremost," said Bruton with a flourish of his hands, "and before we go any further, our trade is to, well, trade. So, if you have something you wish to offer, we can start negotiations."

Jaxson took stock of what they had in their possession. There was nothing they could spare, unfortunately. He reached out to Zero to see if he had any ideas, and Zero reminded Jaxson of the time his dad had dealt with a similar band of traveling traders.

"That might work. Thanks, Zero. Now find someplace to get some rest," Jaxson told Zero, who was circling high above.

"Before I show what I have to offer, I will tell you what I desire," said Jaxson.

Bruton roared with laughter, and all the others in the caravan joined in. Even Jaxson smiled as he waited for a reply. Tam, quiet and watchful, smiled but did not laugh. Bruton looked at Jaxson with a wry grin and said, "That is not how we usually begin, son. But go on now... Tell us what you desire."

"I desire to help keep your Forever Pot plentiful," Jaxson said as he revealed a freshly taken pheasant that had been intended for their supper that night.

"And what do you seek in return?" asked Bruton.

"A bowl to fill our bellies and conversation that leads to friendship," replied Jaxson. His father had said those exact words years ago.

Again, Bruton's laughter rumbled. "There is more to you than there seemed at first glance. Sure, you can help fill the Forever Pot and sup with us around a warm fire tonight!"

The young man stirring the stew that produced the mouthwatering aroma took the pheasant with a slight bow. Bruton guided them around the fire and introduced them as "friends of the dust." After meeting everyone, Jaxson and Tam sat on a log near the fire and listened as the traders bantered with each other before the meal was served. The stew was hot and satisfying, and the bread was white and only slightly stale around the edges. Jaxson laid his head back against the log and looked up at the few stars just appearing in the twilight.

"How does a young man like yourself know how to greet folk such as us?" asked Bruton.

"My dad and I came across a caravan once, years ago," replied Jaxson. "We were just outside of goblin territory, and the traders were very wary. I was amazed at their change in attitude after dad offered them some carrots for the Forever Pot."

"Wonder where he learned it?" asked Bruton.

Jaxson shrugged his shoulders, and the camp became quiet again. The horses, picketed behind the wagons, rustled the grass, and the fire popped sporadically. Even those sounds were subdued by a full belly and a sense of safety that Jaxson had not realized he had missed until that moment.

"You said first we needed to trade. What comes next?" asked Tam from the other side of Jaxson.

"Straight to the point, huh?" said Bruton with a chuckle.

"I don't see the need to tarry when we have places to be," responded Tam.

"Fair enough. Typically, our business would conclude after trading, but young Jaxson here has proved to be a friend of the dust. You can stay with us on the road as long as you would like, provided you pull your own weight. Or you can leave any time you desire."

"We didn't see your wagons all morning, so you must be headed north as we are," said Jaxson. When Bruton nodded, he continued, "I don't see why we shouldn't join you for a time."

"It's settled, then. We will break camp before the rising of the sun and we won't stop until the evening site has been found," said Bruton. "Shake the dust from your clothes and rest well. You are with friends."

****

Over the next few days Jaxson watched the seven-wagon caravan with growing wonder. It was a small group of people: Bruton, his wife Sherrin, and their two adult sons, one of whom was married with a small child. There was also a hired hand and his wife, along with three guards. Each morning before the sun rose, the wagons were packed, the horses hitched, and the camp cleared. Each evening before the last wagon came to a stop, the first was already setting up that night's campsite.

The first wagon contained daily supplies such as pots, pans, dry and preserved foods, and water, among other things. The second was strictly for the horses, filled with feed, oats, extra tack, and harnesses. The next wagon contained cots, bedrolls, extra clothing, and family needs. Jaxson never saw anyone enter or even open the next three wagons, and he assumed the goods intended for trade were stored in them. The final wagon was home to the guards and was in the worse condition by far. When Jaxson asked Bruton about its rough appearance, the large man grunted and shrugged. He made a comment about no one in his family neglecting a wagon like that.

Days later, several hours after sunrise, the caravan came to a fork in the road. Bruton and his family were heading east, so Jaxson and Tam departed their company, though not before some brisk trading.

"We've been together for days! You have nothing of value to trade besides your friendship, and that will not be worth much in goods," said Bruton with a laugh.

Early on just after coming down from the mountains, Jaxson had discussed with Tam that they may need to trade a small piece of the dragon glass Tam had packed away. The air was turning cold, not just due to their trek north but also the coming of winter. Their horses could also use some oats instead of the tough grasses found alongside the road.

"How about we tell you what we are seeking, and if you have any of it, we'll make an offer," said Jaxson.

Bruton opened his hands, palms up, and swept them wide, indicating he was open to trade.

Jaxson nodded. "We have quite the list."

"We are in need of winter coats, traveling food, oats for the horses, and feathers for arrows," said Tam.

Bruton's belly bounced as he chuckled. "And what do you offer in trade?"

"Before we show ours, do you have what we seek?" asked Tam.

"We could accommodate the request easily. But it would tally a gold mark, or at least fourteen silver pieces," replied Bruton with a frown. "Sorry, lads."

"Is that all?" asked Jaxson. "In that case, we also seek information, which can be much more expensive."

Bruton raised an eyebrow. "Indeed. Certain information can be very expensive, but the wagons need to push on. What do you have to trade?"

The large man's eyes bulged when Tam pulled out a hand-sized piece of red glowing dragon glass. His mouth moved but no words passed his lips. Jaxson and Tam smiled.

Tam said, "You think this will do?"

Once Bruton could finally speak, he gestured wildly. "Open the wagons – we're trading today! Boys, all you asked for will be yours, and the finest we have. And any – and I mean *any* – information I can provide. It will be done."

"We want to know about Folja," said Jaxson. "Everything you can tell us. We need a general layout of the city. Where can we go to locate someone within the city? Where do the King's dragons stay? We have many questions."

"We'll travel no farther today. After you select your goods, I will give you my complete attention..." said Bruton. "Once the glass is in my hand, that is."

CHAPTER 28

Much had happened in the five weeks they had been on the road north. Jaxson had spent more time in the saddle of a horse than ever before. They hunted and fished for food, though Tam seemed to favor foraging for berries and edible fruits more with each passing day. Tam had said his taste for meat had not completely gone, but his willingness to hunt for it was slowly seeping away. For the first time in Jaxson's life, he had whiskers. Tam had a full-grown beard, and teased Jaxson about his facial hair from time to time. After another round of his jovial remarks, Jaxson said, "Looks like you're turning into the animals you talk to, with your furry face!"

Tam laughed for the first time in days, and offered to teach Jaxson that night how to shave. Then, as they sat at their little campfire, Tam opened up about his past, something both had avoided doing during their time together.

He was the eldest son of an old and powerful family in Goulage. At one time, the family's reach had extended from the great river in the east to the capital, and down to Goulage. With the town's decline, his father's interests are now closer to home. Tam was expected to take over the family business one day, but he could never see himself sitting behind a desk looking at figures and messages for the rest of his life. So, he spent as little time learning from his father as possible. Most in the town considered him a slacker and a bit of a prankster, though the latter label seemed warranted. Tam told Jaxson that this trip had proved to him that he was meant to be on the road and in the wild, rather than in a town pushing papers.

In turn, Jaxson revealed more about his own past. He spoke

of his father, Alan. How he was a courier of sorts, a seeker of rare items, and a jack of many trades. His father had made powerful friends plying his trade across Kealqua. He also had some strong enemies. Jaxson's mom had died a few years ago from a weak heart. Jaxson didn't elaborate, and Tam didn't push what was a tender subject.

Jaxson had spent most of his time alone with Zero. His dad had travelled extensively and would be gone from their mountain home for weeks or even months at a time. When he came back, he would stay for a while, then go again. Jaxson had no idea where or how his father had acquired Zero's egg. He was just glad that he had. His mom had wanted to be rid of it. She thought a dragon would bring unwanted attention upon them, and that it would eat them out of house and home. She saw no reason to keep a dragon around – until Zero hatched. There had been an instant connection between Jaxson and Zero that his mother couldn't deny. Jaxson didn't talk about his most recent adventures that had spurred him onto his current path, but he did elaborate briefly about Dreknoxious.

The old man was a friend of his father's and had stopped in on them many times over the years. Jaxson always assumed he was a seeker and trader of rare items, like his father. However, the more time he spent with Dreknoxious lately, the more he realized that there was something different about him. He knew things no one should have a right to know and could do things that defied logic. He traveled quickly and never tired. He had a limitless knowledge of almost any subject Jaxson had asked him about. Jaxson couldn't pin down exactly what Dreknoxious was, but he was sure the old man was more than he seemed.

****

"What is your plan?" asked Tam for at least the fifth time in the last few hours.

Jaxson and Zero continued to look out over the Kingdom of Esther from their camp on the ridge high up Mount Fornessor.

Even with all that Bruton had told them about Folja, there was so much they didn't know. Dreknoxious had told Jaxson that his father may be in the city, but was concerned he may have been in trouble. Should Jaxson start by looking in the prisons? What if he was dead? How would he know?

Too many questions. His shoulders sagged. "I don't know."

"We can't stay up here forever. We came to find your father... let's get to it," said Tam.

"He is correct. We cannot help your father from here," said Zero.

"Both of you are right, of course," said Jaxson. "Tomorrow. We will go into the city tomorrow."

"And..." prompted Tam.

"I'll locate Dreknoxious's contact in the palace gardens. Perhaps he can tell us where to start," said Jaxson. "And Zero, I want you to stay up here. I'll check out the dragon keep and make sure all we need is the crest."

Zero's large nostrils flared.

"I know you don't like it, but it's easier for me to blend in riding a horse rather than an almost full-grown dragon!"

Tam studied Zero for a moment. When the dragon settled down, he said, "Tomorrow it is, then."

CHAPTER 29

The horses' hooves clomping down the dirt path were the only sounds in the predawn stillness. Jaxson and Tam had left the camp on the mountainside hours earlier, striking south in order to approach the city on the main road and not from the direction of the Triplets. Jaxson strained his eyes but could see very little as the stars were shrouded, and the sun provided only a faint glow on the horizon. He focused instead on listening for anything unusual, but that too proved fruitless, as all he could hear was the steady cadence of the horses.

Unlike most major roads leading to other major cities, the thoroughfare to Folja had no merchants and was not lined with inns. There were no bazaars or open markets. There was nothing to distract travelers from the view of the castle and the older and larger dragon keep behind it. The sun had risen fully by the time the duo had passed the farms and saw the capital of the Kingdom of Esther for the first time.

Jaxson, wide-eyed and mouth open, stared toward the black and blood-red stone of the castle. He saw the sweeping walls, impossibly high and dotted with archer's nests and the occasional tower. Behind the castle, sat the enormous, smooth dragon's keep. The buildings, which did not rival the Temple of Greeti within the Taufan, were not what caught Jaxson's full attention, however. Throngs of people moved in all directions. Lines of people streamed into the palace. Another steady flow of bodies moved out of the castle's gate, walking toward the market. Guards, dozens and dozens, marched along the tops of the walls. Men guiding carts with vegetables, hay, and scraps jockeyed for position along the road leading to the city. There were more people in Jaxson's view now than he had ever seen in his whole life.

"I know the plan was to split up, but…" began Tam. "If you aren't sure?"

Jaxson pulled his eyes away from the masses and looked at Tam. "No. No, I'll be fine."

Tam shook his head. "Then I'm headed to the market. News and rumors flow like water in places like that."

Jaxson didn't respond. Instead, his eyes followed a group of armored soldiers as they marched out of the castle gates and beyond view along the wall.

"Look, come with me until we get a grasp on what we are dealing with in the city," said Tam.

"I guess," replied Jaxson. He raised his chin and straightened his shoulders. "First the market, and then to the gardens to meet Dreknoxious's contact."

"I'll do all the talking," said Tam.

Jaxson rolled his eyes, but was secretly relieved. "Just remember, we're here for my father… His name is Alan Alpine, and he has a long scar on his neck."

****

After the chaotic swirl of bodies, sounds, and smells of the marketplace, Jaxson enjoyed the tranquility of the palace gardens. Lanes and paths wound through a maze of spectacular flowers and budding trees. The rich and vibrant colors were second only to the pleasant, mingled aromas of the flowers, grasses, and fertilizers, which massaged the nose instead of punching it, like the smells of the marketplace.

Jaxson closed his eyes and reached out to Zero. Over the period traveling north to the capital, they had worked on maintaining contact over longer and longer distances. Despite this training, all they could communicate to each other this far apart were feelings. As soon as Jaxson reached out for Zero, impatience and boredom crashed into him. He laughed out loud and sent back safe and positive thoughts.

Tam walked beside him as they ambled along the lanes.

"What did that last merchant tell you?" asked Jaxson.

Tam snuck a peek at Jaxson from the corner of his eye, then laughed. "If your face hadn't been buried in that pot of rice and greens, maybe you'd have heard." He smiled, but Jaxson could see no mirth in his eyes. He had heard something that troubled him, that much was clear. Jaxson was only unsure why Tam didn't share his findings.

He stopped suddenly as a sweet, nourishing sensation washed over him. He turned and was drawn into a circular court-yard surrounded by high walls. Vines, covered in tiny pink and yellow flowers, grew thickly from the ground to the tops of the walls. Smells of spring and honey and fresh grass filled the small space. The air buzzed as hundreds of tiny hummingbirds darted along the vines, getting their fill of nectar.

A giggle escaped Jaxson's lips. Here within the courtyard he was renewed, strong, ready. He threw his head back and his arms out, and twirled around, soaking in the energy the tiny birds passed to him.

"What did you say?" he said, coming out of his revelry.

Tam shook his head. "I said... Remind me how we are sup-posed to find this contact of Dreknoxious's?"

"Oh, right. We need to find a gardener and ask where to find the yellow moon flowers," replied Jaxson.

Tam pointed at a small woman tending the vines on the other side of the raised platform in the center of the courtyard. "What about her? Looks like she works here."

"She will do," said Jaxson.

CHAPTER 30

The baggy robes of the gardener tending the vines did little to hide how small she was. Jaxson approached her from behind and cleared his throat. She whirled around quickly, her spade held like a knife to defend herself. Jaxson noticed she appeared older than he had at first thought. She was closer to Tam's twenty years than his sixteen. The dirt smeared on her cheeks only added to the threat presented by the spade.

Jaxson raised his hands and backed away slowly. "Whoa now! Didn't mean to scare you," he said.

The gardener looked down at the spade and blushed. She quickly put it away and said, "Why were you sneaking up on me like that?"

"I wasn't sneaking," said Jaxson. "In fact, I came seeking help."

Her eyes narrowed. "What kind of help?"

"We – myself and my friend over there—" Jaxson indicated Tam, "—are interested in seeing the moon flower. We hear this garden has some?"

"Is this some kind of joke?" said the woman. She looked around expectantly. "Did Rockus put you up to this?"

Jaxson and Tam exchanged confused glances. "No joke," Jaxson said. "We're looking for the moon flower."

Her smile was replaced by an impatient scowl. She pointed to the platform behind them. "The moon flowers are in the raised bed on that platform there. You walked right past them."

Jaxson looked back to the small platform. In a stone bed grew a lush green bush which spilled over the edge. On each side, blossomed the largest white flowers he had ever seen, easily bigger than both of his hands put together. They were snow white, a darker cream color near the center. Even from this distance, Jaxson could see the outline of a star within each flower.

"You got any yellow ones?" asked Tam from behind Jaxson.

"Not many people come to the royal gardens seeking a fairy tale," said the woman. "Why do you?"

Jaxson took a step closer. "An old friend told us to seek them out in this garden."

"Does this friend have a name?" she asked.

Jaxson glanced at Tam, who nodded. "Dreknoxious."

The woman made no indication that she had heard him. She stared at Jaxson without moving. Just before Jaxson was going to repeat the name, she said, "Finally! You must be Jaxson, and that makes you Tam. My name is Aleera."

"Great to meet you!" said Jaxson.

"Yes, well met, but I thought it would be more difficult to find our contact," said Tam.

"I have stayed near the moon flowers since Dreknoxious told me to expect you two," replied Aleera.

Jaxson nodded. "That makes sense. So, where is the old man?"

Aleera sighed. "Dreknoxious passed this way over a week ago. He did not stay long."

It was Jaxson's turn to sigh. He ran his hand through his long hair. "I can never find the man when I need him."

"He expected your arrival weeks ago. He thought he was the one showing up late," said Aleera.

"It took us longer than we would have liked," said Tam. "What's our plan now, Jaxson?"

Before Jaxson could reply, Aleera interjected. "I have no idea when Dreknoxious may return, but he did tell me some about your search. I know you seek your father, Jaxson. I may be able to help you."

"How can you help?" asked Tam.

"Do you think a man like Dreknoxious would trust me if I

had no skills of my own?" asked Aleera.

"That doesn't really answer the question," replied Tam. Aleera glared at him, and Tam stared right back.

"Come on. Everybody can help," said Jaxson. "What do we do now?"

Aleera pulled her gaze away from Tam. "I have a few ideas."

"I do as well," said Tam, though he never took his eyes off of Aleera. "I'm going to start by checking the dungeons."

"And I can gain access to the palace. I'll start there," said Aleera.

"Now we're getting somewhere," said Jaxson. "I'm going to look around the dragon keep. I need to learn everything about the place, so I can bring Zero back with me."

"How are you going to get into the dungeons?" asked Aleera.

Tam sneered. "Don't worry about it. I'll get eyes down there."

"I hope you don't find him down there," said Jaxson. "Aleera, my dad's name is Alan Alpine. He's tall and thin, like me. He also has a rough scar on his neck. I don't want to talk too much about why he was here, but I know he doesn't like everything that's going on, especially with the dragons."

Jaxson didn't notice Aleera start at the mention of a scar, but he saw Tam looking in her direction. He seemed to have been watching Aleera closely, as if to gauge her reaction to Jaxson's description. *It doesn't matter. Stay focused,* Jaxson told himself. The sun had crossed the midday zenith, but there was still plenty of time in the day.

"Where do we meet after?" asked Tam.

Jaxson shrugged and looked to Aleera.

"There is an inn near the docks, known as Sea Critters," said Aleera. "Its real name, which is on the sign, is The Turtle, the Seahorse and the Octopus. It has adequate enough rooms, and sailors from the ships are always in and out. They're loud and haven't bathed in weeks... You two should fit right in."

CHAPTER 31

As he walked out of the gardens and around the castle's outer wall, all the way around to the dragon's keep, Jaxson imagined many ways to get into the keep. Each scheme was more elaborate and ridiculous than the previous one. Even while he was planning his entry, he devoted part of his attention to avoiding large, uncomfortable crowds. He stayed close to the castle wall, as most seemed to give the castle a wide berth. He was deep in thought when he rounded a corner and found the dragon keep looming over him.

The stone keep predated the castle by hundreds of years. It was from another time when dragons and their dragonriders were revered, and in turn, the dragonriders and their dragons kept the kingdom safe. There were no dragonriders now, only people that rode dragons by force or by controlling them somehow. Jaxson often wished he had the magic of the dragonriders of old. They were said to rival even the great wizards of their time.

The large stones were interlocked tightly without mortar. Age had turned them dark black on the lower levels, fading to a lighter gray above. Large, gateless openings encircled each floor, offering safe landing places for dragons, except at the bottommost floor, which was solid stone, with the exception of the service entrances and one conventional gate not large enough for a dragon to squeeze through. Jaxson stared in wonder as a large crimson dragon, riderless, landed on the third level and scampered inside, head low.

Guards wearing the colors of the King of Esther circled the keep and stood watch at the gate. After watching for some time and still no closer to finding a way in, Jaxson decided to take a closer look at the gate. He tiptoed along the rubble alongside a dilapidated building, approaching the gate slowly.

Then he heard sounds of a chase from behind him. He saw the guards first, then a scruffy, small boy of twelve years shot past him. The boy tried to turn toward the keep but slipped on some loose rocks. The guards would be on top of him within moments. Without thinking, Jaxson rushed to the boy and shoved him behind a pile of broken barrels. He waved at the guards and pointed back towards the castle, yelling that the boy had gone that way. The two winded guards turned and jogged in the opposite direction.

Moments later, the brown-haired boy popped up. "Thought my goose was cooked for sure that time."

"Why were they chasing you?" asked Jaxson.

"I thought they had too many apples in their sack," said the boy, revealing two large, red apples from somewhere in his loose shirt. "What made you help me?"

Jaxson thought for a moment. "I saw no risk in it. If I hadn't helped you, they would have caught you, no doubt. But... by helping you, I could find out why two guards were so eagerly pursuing a small boy. If I needed to, I could turn you in myself."

"And are you going to do that?" asked the boy. He slowly started inching behind the barrels again.

"I don't see any reason to get all worked up over a couple of apples. My name is Jaxson. What's yours?"

"My friends call me Mica. Thanks for the help, but I have to be getting to work," said the boy as he brushed off his pants.

"I won't hold you up then," said Jaxson. He backed up and allowed Mica to return to the dusty street.

"Great! I can't be late again. Griz'll whip me and let me go this time. Mucking out the dwellings isn't much fun, but it puts coin in my purse." Mica started walking toward the dragon keep, and Jaxson fell in step beside him.

"Do you work at the keep?" he asked.

"Of course, I do. Where else are there any dragon dwellings that need tending?"

"I'm not sure what a dwelling is," replied Jaxson.

"I guess they're big stables for the dragons," said Mica. "But everyone knows that. You aren't from here, are you?"

"I am not," said Jaxson. "Think ol' Griz would hire me to help around the dwellings?"

Mica looked Jaxson up and down, then smiled. "Probably. There's always more work than hands to get it done. Come along, and we'll find out."

****

Jaxson followed the boy through a service door of the keep and into a low-ceilinged, crowded room. Boys and young men shuffled around, waiting to receive their assigned dragon dwelling to clear out and service. Everyone grew quiet as a short man hobbled into the room from a doorway at the far side. He walked with an odd gait, and Jaxson noticed he had one wooden leg. Half of the man's face was a melted scar, except around his lips, which were perfect as his teeth when he gave the group a large smile.

"That's Griz," said Mica quietly. "He'll be giving out the orders. Some of us will help bring up food for the dragons. Some will be assigned to the riders' area cleaning, cooking, and stuff. I'm hoping to draw one of the dragon dwellings. Afternoons are easy if the dragons aren't here, and most of the time they aren't."

"What do new guys get to do?" asked Jaxson.

"Mostly cleaning duty. You'll sweep the halls, or something like that."

Griz turned his gnarled head towards Jaxson and Mica. "You new, then?"

Jaxson nodded. "I am—"

"Fine. You don't know better, but keep your mouth shut while assignments are being given," growled Griz.

"No need for all that, Griz," said Mica.

Griz focused on the small boy, and Mica wilted. "*You* should know better, boy! No easy job for you today. You get Blackthorn's Dwell."

A collective gasp came from the boys in the room. Now everyone was looking at Mica with a mix of fear and dread.

"You wouldn't," replied Mica.

"Might teach you some respect," said Griz with an impish smile. "Oh, and the morning crew didn't make it up there. The dwell hasn't been mucked in a couple of days. Should be ripe."

Mica's face turned white, and he appeared to be sick. Jaxson leaned close and whispered, "Are you unwell?"

Griz's attention snapped to Jaxson. "You don't learn too fast, do you? You can join him!"

Before Jaxson could respond, Mica pulled him to a stairway at the back of the room. They were halfway up the stairs before Mica said, "Bad luck, but we should be all right. Maybe Blackthorn won't be in the dwell. We'll muck it good and get out. With two of us, it shouldn't take long."

"Why is everyone scared of Blackthorn?" asked Jaxson.

"He's a nasty, protective dragon. He don't like folks in his dwell, ever. But he's pleasant compared to his rider, Grayton. That is one foul fella," replied Mica.

"That doesn't sound good," said Jaxson.

Mica shook his head and kept climbing. "Nothing for it but to do it. We'll get through it. Just keep our heads down and hurry. Like I said, maybe Blackthorn won't be around."

CHAPTER 32

Jaxson's chest heaved and his boots felt as though they were filled with water as he slogged up the final steps to the top of the dragon keep. Mica, unlike Jaxson, appeared unfazed by the climb. He put his hand on the door handle leading to Blackthorn's dwelling, and his shoulders tensed. When he opened the door slightly, Jaxson didn't have to see inside to know it was empty: Mica's shoulders dropped, and he let out a deep sigh. He turned to Jaxson and giggled. "Come on, let's get to work."

The spacious dwelling was surprisingly clean. Jaxson looked all around the room for something to "muck," but he only saw a large pile of stones along the far wall. Near the back of the dwell, wooden doors were set into the floor, and he saw a small area filled with items such as buckets, mops, and brooms.

"Mica, I thought this place would be messier, the way everyone talked about how disgusting mucking a dwell can be," said Jaxson.

Mica looked around for a moment, his brow furrowed. Then he smiled and said, "You're thinking of horse stables, right?"

"Yeah, I guess," replied Jaxson.

"Dragons aren't as simple or as dumb as horses. They do that type of business outside their dwell."

"So, what are we to do?" asked Jaxson.

"We have quite the list. Follow me, and we'll get started. With the tiny gods on our side, we'll be long gone before Blackthorn or Grayton come back."

He led Jaxson to the rocks and around the rear. Even before they turned the corner, Jaxson's nose filled with the stench of rotting and charred flesh. Bones, cracked and burnt, littered the floor behind the stone barrier. Although there was very little meat, what was left had clearly been sitting there for days. Worms and bugs crawled all over it. Jaxson turned away quickly.

"Come on, it's not that bad. I've seen worse," said Mica, giving him a pat on the back. He pointed toward the far wall. "Take this broom and start sweeping the stuff that way."

Mica walked over to the trapdoors and jerked on a thick rope attached to the wall. The doors dropped open with a loud bang. Jaxson started shoving the remains of the dragon's meal toward the opening in the floor. Mica grabbed a wheelbarrow filled with a bluish powder and followed behind, dusting the floor liberally. Several smelly, sweaty trips later, the remains were down the hatch, and the floor was covered in blue powder. *Smells better already,* thought Jaxson as he leaned heavily on his broom.

"No rest for the weary," said Mica. He held two mops and a bucket filled with water. "Still quite a bit to get done."

"Can we take a break?" asked Jaxson.

"After we clear this cleanse powder."

After an hour of work, mopping and slogging the bucket back and forth, the floor was clean once more. Jaxson sat on one of the rocks and laid his head back. Mica put away their cleaning supplies and came to join him.

"We might just get finished in time," said Mica.

Jaxson nodded. After a moment, he asked, "Mica, how do dragons get a dwelling?"

Mica had pulled out a hard piece of bread from somewhere in his ratty clothes. He replied, "Don't know. Don't care."

"Do you know if there are any empty ones?"

Mica looked at Jaxson out of the corner of his eye. "A few. Why?"

"No reason."

"Break's over, question boy. Let's sweep out Blackthorn's landing," said Mica.

****

Hours later, drenched in sweat, both boys leaned against the outer wall overlooking the Laguza Sea. A cool breeze danced across Jaxson's tired body and tickled his sweaty neck. The orange sun was almost touching the horizon to the west. He was tired and knew he was going to be sore in the morning.

"All we have to do is get the dragon's meal up here, and we'll be finished," said Mica.

"Are you ready?" asked Jaxson.

"Not just yet... This view almost makes it worth it. You ever been to the mountains on the other side of the Laguza?"

"No. I have been in mountains, just not those," replied Jaxson.

"I want to see the mountains one day. See 'em really up close."

"Mica, does the keep ever get dragon visitors? Dragons that don't live here?"

"Some riders live way off and only come by occasionally, if that's what you mean," said Mica.

"Where do those dragons stay?" asked Jaxson.

"You ask a lot of questions..." Mica sighed. "The other three dwellings on this level are empty. They say it's to have room for guests, but I think no one wants to be near Grayton and Blackthorn."

"Why is everyone so scared of those two?"

"I hope you never have to find out," said Mica. "Come on, let's get the meat up here and then get out."

The boys turned and walked back into the dwell. Halfway to the trapdoor, the room went dark. Jaxson turned and his mouth dropped open. In the opening stood Blackthorn, larger than any dragon Jaxson had ever seen, blocking the fading sunlight.

"That's not good," said Mica.

CHAPTER 33

Mica grabbed Jaxson's shoulder and whispered in his ear, "Stay quiet, and come with me."

Jaxson followed the scruffy boy back to the trapdoor and then beyond it. For the first time, he noticed other doors in the wall, of varying sizes. Mica opened one of the small ones at eye level. Jaxson saw it was filled with taut ropes running up and down.

"Was Grayton with him?" asked Mica as he yanked on several of the ropes.

"I think there was a rider. That would be Grayton, right?"

"Tiny gods help us," said Mica. He tugged several other ropes, some twice and others just once, then back to the first for two more tugs.

"What are you…"

"No time to explain. It's how the people in the kitchen know to send us meals for both a dragon and a rider," said Mica.

His eyes bulged as he turned to look back to the landing. Blackthorn, large and charcoal black, walked into the dwell. He looked around and then dipped down to allow Grayton to slide from his back. Once Grayton was on the ground, Blackthorn turned and laid on the landing, looking out at the sunset. Jaxson was impressed with Grayton's light but ornate armor. A silver breastplate over a supple leather shirt offered some protection but great mobility. He carried a longsword at his belt with a large emerald at the end of the hilt. His weapon and armor were immaculate, but Jaxson thought Grayton himself looked like he needed a bath. He wasn't exactly dirty, but greasy.

"Where's my food, boy?" boomed Grayton.

Mica bowed low. "On the way now, sir."

Grayton grunted and walked through a doorway. Beyond, Jaxson saw a small room with a sitting chair and a table with only a bench. Mica followed and poured wine into the only glass. After the bounty hunter was seated at the table with glass in hand, Mica came back out to check for the food. He opened another small door next to the one with the ropes. It was empty. Mica stuck his head inside to look down the shaft. Then he started yanking the ropes again, now with more urgency. After a few moments, the ropes jerked in response. Mica wiped his brow and smiled at Jaxson.

Jaxson moved beside the boy and looked into the second door. The smell of roasted meat wafted up the shaft. He could see a plate laden with meat, potatoes, and bread rising up to meet them. Mica pulled the plate through the door and turned to deliver it to Grayton.

"Oof," said Mica with a start. Grayton stood right behind them with his arms crossed.

The plate tumbled out of Mica's hands and landed on the tall bounty hunter's boots.

A smile flashed across Grayton's face just before his hand slashed out. Mica's head jerked to the side, and he tumbled to the floor, holding his bloodied cheek. Jaxson saw Blackthorn raise his head and his nostrils flare, but then he simply turned back to the sunset.

Grayton pulled back his foot to kick the fallen boy. Jaxson jumped in between them.

"My apologies, sir! Let me clean your boots while Mica gets you a fresh plate," he said. He knelt and started unlacing Grayton's boots before the bounty hunter could object.

"Fine. But be quick about it," said Grayton. He kicked off his dirty boots, then strutted into the sitting room.

Jaxson helped Mica to his feet and wiped the blood away. "The cut isn't bad, but you're going to have a whopping black eye."

"Don't worry about it," said Mica, swiping Jaxson's hand away. "Be quiet and get to work, or it'll be worse."

He returned to pulling on ropes, then cleaned up the spilled food. Jaxson saw Mica eat as much as he threw down the shaft. Footsteps behind Jaxson made him double down on the boot cleaning.

"Never seen you around here before, boy," said Grayton.

"No sir. I'm not from the city," said Jaxson without rising from his work.

Grayton grunted and paced around. "At least you show some respect. You aren't as dumb as this one," he said, pointing at Mica, "or the dragons. They have to be made to show respect."

Jaxson snarled but kept cleaning the boots. Grayton ambled off just as the ropes started jerking again. Mica pulled out a fresh plate of food and delivered it to the bounty hunter, who wasted no time in tearing into the steaming meat. Jaxson finished the boots, and as he placed his hands on the floor to help him stand, there was something squishy under his fingers. Maggots squirmed out of a chunk of putrid meat that they must have missed while cleaning up. Without a thought, Jaxson jammed the smelly meat deep into one of Grayton's boots.

As Mica exited the sitting room, Grayton yelled, "Bring my boots here, boy!"

Jaxson brought the boots to the bounty hunter, bowed, and exited as quickly as possible. As he passed Mica, he whispered, "We need to go, now."

The boys were almost to the stairs when they heard Grayton scream.

"Run!" yelled Jaxson.

"I'm gonna kill you, boy!" Grayton yelled as the boys fled down the stairs as fast as they could.

CHAPTER 34

Jaxson followed closely as Mica raced down the stairwell, sometimes taking two or three steps at a time. Mica was faster than him, but Jaxson was determined not to get left behind. When Mica came to a sudden stop on a landing just above the bottom floor, Jaxson crashed into him at full speed. Both boys hit the ground hard but were on their feet in seconds. Jaxson started down the stairwell that led to the room where all the boys gathered to get their assignments, but Mica stopped him.

"We can't…" he said, still taking in haggard breaths, "go that way."

"What? Why?" asked Jaxson, bent double with his hands on his knees. "Isn't that the way out of here?"

"It is. But if Grayton hopped on Blackthorn, that's right where he'll be waiting," said Mica.

"You're probably right. Where to, then?"

Mica looked around. "There aren't many routes to choose from, and each has its own risks. I think we should go out by the kitchens. We can cover ourselves in flour or something. But to get there, we have to go right beside the armorer."

"Is that bad?" asked Jaxson.

"It's where the dragons' armor is made, and if rumors are true, where sorcerers imbue it with magic," said Mica. His eyes were wide, and his head was twitching from side to side. Jaxson thought he looked like a startled deer. The slightest noise would make him bolt.

"Is that still the best way to avoid Grayton?" he asked.

Mica nodded.

"That's our plan, then. We can do this. Now, lead the way."

"Well, we can't go down," said Mica. "This way. Follow me."

He ran along a hall with no doors, stopping frequently to listen for trouble. Jaxson stayed close, but not as close as he had on the stairs, his head still thumped from their collision. As they approached an intersection, Mica indicated they should stop.

"I've never been this far, but I'm fairly confident we need to go right," he said.

"Let's do it, then," said Jaxson, starting down the hall to the right.

Mica grabbed his shoulder and pulled him back.

"Not so fast. We need to be careful. The armorer is down that hall. Stay quiet, and if we're seen, run."

Jaxson nodded. It would be a dreadful way to end his quest to find his dad: caught by some magic armor-makers in a place he should never have been. He hoped Tam and Aleera were having better luck than him. Calming his mind, he sent a nervously confident thought to Zero.

"Why are you nervous?" Zero said in his head.

"Why are you so close? Where are you?" asked Jaxson.

"Don't worry. I am above the thick clouds above the city. No one can see me," replied Zero. *"Now, why are you so nervous?"*

"No time to explain. We, Mica and me – he's a boy I just met – have to sneak past some magic-wielding armor-makers to escape a pissed off bounty hunter in the dragon keep."

"Do you need me?"

"I do. But right now, I need you to stay out of sight and be safe. I'll let you know if things get out of hand."

"Jaxson! Can you hear me?" asked Mica.

"I can. Sorry, I was just thinking," said Jaxson.

"Come on," said Mica as he started down the hall.

The hall was straighter and narrower than their previous path. Doors lined the right-hand side and every twenty steps on the left was a small window. They were halfway along the hall when Jaxson first noticed a tingling running all through his body. It was the familiar sensation he knew from the times he and Zero had used their skill to heal someone. Yet, this time it was foreign in a way that was difficult to describe. It was cold and wrong. Each step he took, the sensation became stronger until he couldn't take it anymore. He had to see what was causing it.

The door was a single solid piece of wood interrupted only by a circular handle. His hand vibrated when he grasped the handle and pulled. From somewhere far behind him, Mica pulled on his shoulder, and he heard him pleading for them to keep moving. When the door finally cracked open, Mica fled.

Jaxson was horrified. Inside the room was a young dragon strapped down with many heavy chains – though, in its pitiful condition, the restraints seemed unnecessary. Robed and hooded figures stood around the dragon, chanting in a language Jaxson did not understand. Two others were holding a sigil – like the one Jaxson and Tam had found in the forest – beneath a wound in the dragon's side. The final robed figure pulled a long dagger, expanding the wound. As the blood of the dragon landed on the sigil, steam rose and a hissing sound filled the room.

Jaxson locked eyes with the dragon and deep anguish and hopelessness washed over him. He tried to tell the dragon he would help, and opened the door wider. Suddenly, the dragon's head snapped up and he looked right at Jaxson.

"RUN!"

And Jaxson ran. He ran from the robed figures. He ran from the plight of the dragon. Most of all, he ran because he was not ready to confront that type of evil; he could barely comprehend it. Using dragon's blood in magic to control other dragons – that was the only way the bounty hunters could control their dragons. Jaxson felt ill as he stumbled into the kitchen. Mica braced him and led him through the doorway into the night air.

"Sea Critters Inn," he mumbled to Mica before passing out.

CHAPTER 35

Dusty cobwebs stretched between the wooden rafters of the low ceiling. Jaxson watched a spider scurry quick as lightning across its web to trap a fly. Nothing in his head was working so fast. His thoughts were jumbled. The last thing he remembered was the overwhelming crush of dread and defeat coming from the chained dragon in the keep. The edges of his vision started darkening again.

"You back with us?" asked Tam.

Jaxson tried to turn his head to see Tam, but settled back on the bed instead. "I guess," he said.

"What happened?"

He forced himself to sit up. After opening and closing his eyes several times, his head cleared. "I was able to get into the keep," he said, looking around the room. "Where's Mica?"

"The boy? He dropped you off and ran," replied Tam. "Haven't seen him since."

Jaxson took tiny sips from the cup Tam offered. The water was cool. The bread had been fresh two days ago, but still Jaxson attempted to nibble at it. His thoughts strayed back to the captured dragon. He could never imagine Zero being held in chains and drained of his blood like that.

ZERO!

"Are you nearby?" asked Jaxson.

"I am still high above you," replied Zero. *"Are you well? I have been worried."*

"I'm with Tam now. I should be fine," said Jaxson.

"Good. I need to rest. I will be back at Mount Fornessor. Stay

well."

Jaxson smiled. At least Zero was unharmed and hadn't tried to storm the keep.

"How long have I been asleep?" he asked Tam.

"Through the night and most of today," replied Tam.

Jaxson was amazed that Zero had stayed aloft for that long. With his head cleared and strength returning, he asked, "Did you find anything about my dad?"

Before Tam could answer, a long, furry worm with legs leapt into his lap. It was wiggling and moving rapidly, causing Tam to laugh and shout. "Move off now, Sugar. I'll get you a treat in a minute."

"What in the name of the tiny gods is that thing?" asked Jaxson with a smile on his face.

"This here is a ferret. She's crazy about the sugar cubes horse trainers use on their mounts. Hence her name. She's rambunctious, but sweet and helpful. She even helped check the dungeons for your father."

"And..." Jaxson trailed off.

"Your dad isn't there," said Tam.

"That's great! Have you heard from Aleera?"

"I have. She should be back any minute. I know she didn't find much – but Jaxson, I need to tell you something." Tam put Sugar on the ground with a few sugar cubes to keep her busy. "I saw the leader of the Death Cult. They're the ones controlling the dragons. I overheard him telling some rough-looking guys to bleed the winged beast dry, and then get rid of it."

"That's horrible. And I think I know what he was talking about," said Jaxson.

"Hold on. The man, the leader, he was tall and thin, with—"

There was a soft tap at the door, then it opened slowly. An old man with a gnarled, wooden staff slowly entered the room with Aleera in tow.

"Dreknoxious!" exclaimed Jaxson. "You're here."

"I found him nosing around the gardens looking for you two," said Aleera with a smile. "So, I brought him straight here."

"We have much to discuss... much, much to discuss – but first, do you have anything to eat?" asked Dreknoxious, eyeing Jaxson's bread and licking his lips.

After consuming anything edible in the room including some of Sugar's horse treats, Dreknoxious settled on the end of Jaxson's bed and looked at the group before him.

"I am so glad to see that you boys are safe. When you did not arrive in Folja before me, I feared the road north had become more dangerous than I had anticipated," he said. His warm smile spread to the others. "And you met Aleera! The little tip about the moonflowers played out, I see. Now, is there any word on Alan?"

Tam looked at Jaxson and started to speak. Jaxson beat him to it. "No, we have been able to ask around with the merchants, check the dungeons, and Aleera checked the palace today. You didn't find anything, did you?"

Aleera shook her head, so Jaxson continued, "Not even a whisper."

Dreknoxious's brow furrowed, and he closed his eyes. When he opened them again, he looked at Jaxson. "I am truly sorry I could not wait for your arrival. There were pressing matters to the west that needed my immediate attention."

Jaxson tilted his head. "What kind of pressing matters?"

"It is a humorous but sad tale for another time, I am afraid. I do need to impress something upon the three of you," Dreknoxious leaned in, looking at each of the three young people in turn. "The problems facing the dragons, the people of Folja, and the Kingdom of Esther are just a glimpse of a bigger issue. I don't have all the answers yet, only bits and pieces, but it's enough to indicate that something drastic is happening right under our noses."

"What do you mean by that?" asked Tam.

"I have said all I am going to say before I hear from you two. Aleera filled me in on all she knew on the way here," said the old man. "Tam, you searched the dungeons? Anything turn up, besides human suffering and depravity?"

Tam looked from Dreknoxious to Jaxson and back. "Nothing out of the ordinary in the dungeons. I did see the leader of the

DLDC, and he was talking about torturing dragons or something."

"That is troubling news. Jaxson?"

Jaxson recounted all he saw in the dragon keep, from how Mica had helped him get in, to Blackthorn, to Grayton, to his eventual escape after seeing the chained dragon. Dreknoxious asked many questions about the captured dragon and the room in which it was held. As the old man asked more and more probing questions, Jaxson realized he had seen more than he had realized. Dreknoxious seemed particularly interested in the robed figures.

"Could you see any part of their bodies?"

"I told you I couldn't," replied Jaxson.

"What about the hand holding the blade? Did you see it?"

Jaxson thought back to the dagger ripping down the side of the chained dragon. "No, all I can remember is blood."

"Did their heads seem to be shaped like normal heads?"

"Their heads? They were in full robes! But yes, I guess they were normal," said Jaxson, throwing his hands up. "What does that have to do with anything?"

"This is important. Think. Think only about the robed figures... Did anything seem different about them?" asked Dreknoxious.

Jaxson replayed the whole scene in his head. He attempted to avoid focusing on the dragon. The three standing around him seemed off. Why was that? They had their hands raised, but their arms were too long, and their elbows bent the wrong way.

Jaxson relayed this to Dreknoxious. The old man sighed and sagged heavily onto the bed, bracing himself with one hand.

"Vile sorcerers from the Isles of Creptin. The rumors are true," said Dreknoxious.

"Who are they?" asked Jaxson.

"Beings to avoid," he said with a dismissive wave. "Anything else?"

Jaxson looked at his feet for a few moments then up at Dreknoxious. "Well, I think I have a plan to rescue that dragon, and with you here, it might just work. I'll have to go get Zero, of course. He will need a rider to be allowed into the dwellings even with a sigil."

Dreknoxious, Tam, and Aleera listened to Jaxson's plan. After a spirited debate with input from all three, and alterations to the original plan, they had a course of action. Dreknoxious told them to wait one day and then strike that night. Jaxson agreed, as he needed time to rest and contact Zero. The old man left with a promise to return the next day at sundown.

"But what about the search for your dad?" asked Aleera. "If we do this, we'll have to leave – it doesn't matter if we are successful or not."

"My dad saved Zero as an egg," replied Jaxson. "I know he'd want me to save this dragon too."

CHAPTER 36

The cool air blew through Jaxson's hair as he soared high above Folja. Zero slid effortlessly from wind current to wind current as they waited for the signal that it was time to enter the keep. Zero wore the sigil they had found in the woods in the hope that it would keep anyone who might notice them from becoming suspicious. Neither of them liked how it had been made, but it didn't seem to effect Zero at all.

Jaxson had left the city early that morning to meet Zero near Mount Fornessor and inform him of the plan. By now, Tam and Aleera should be in the keep, and Dreknoxious should be preparing the distraction about which he seemed so giddy. Jaxson chuckled as he recalled how the old man's eyes had lit up when he said, "Don't worry about it. I have a few ways to turn some heads."

"*What exactly did Dreknoxious say about the sorcerers?*" asked Zero for the third time.

"*He didn't say anything, really,*" replied Jaxson. "*Just that they were bad. I think that he suspected they were here. Are you ready for this?*"

"*I am. When the signal is lit, we wait for Dreknoxious's distraction. Then we go in.*"

"*That's it. Pretty simple – until we get in there.*"

"*We will worry about that when the time comes,*" said Zero. "*Are you sure we should be doing this?*"

"*I don't see any other choice.*"

"*But what about your father?*"

Jaxson looked down to the keep and thought of all that had happened since he and Zero had left their mountain home in search of his missing father. He was still no closer to finding his father than he had been when he started.

"*It's the right thing to do,*" he said.

Moments later, Zero said, "*There's the signal.*"

Jaxson looked down, but all he could see was a tiny orange dot near to the bottom of the dark keep. "*I'll have to take your word for it.*"

"*What will Dreknoxious do now?*" asked Zero.

"*He said we'd know when we saw it,*" replied Jaxson.

To the south, over the farmland beyond the city walls, dragon's fire erupted across the sky, illuminating dozens of steam drakes flying toward the city. Jaxson could hear their piercing shrieks even from this distance. The sound reminded him of their perilous escape from the large pack of drakes, which had eventually forced them into the Bend.

Again, the dragon's fire lit the sky. Alarms sounded within the castle and the keep. Soldiers spilled out of the barracks to line the walls. Dragons and their riders took off from the keep to meet the drakes.

This was the distraction, and it was working beautifully. Jaxson had no idea how Dreknoxious had accomplished it, but the keep was emptying and all eyes were looking south.

Zero started his descent as dragon's fire lit the sky once more. Tollison, the huge, red dragon, was chasing the drakes toward the city. Jaxson thought he saw Dreknoxious on his back, waving his staff. Then he heard clearly, although the distance should have been too great, Dreknoxious yell, "To arms! Defend the city!"

Their angle of descent was steep, and when Zero's feet finally struck the landing outside the room in which the chained dragon was being held, Jaxson was relieved. The gate had been opened, and Tam greeted him as he slid off Zero's back.

"No problems?" asked Jaxson.

"None. It was just like Dreknoxious said," replied Tam. "No one on the bottom floor stopped us, and we haven't seen anyone on this floor."

"Where's Aleera?"

"Over there, working on the chain," said Tam. "This dragon's in rough shape. I don't think it can fly even if we get him free."

Aleera jogged over. Her face was pale, and her lips were thin lines. "It's only one chain wrapped around it several times. I've picked the lock, but I need help moving it. It's so heavy."

"You can pick locks?" asked Tam.

Aleera was looking back at the dragon and didn't respond.

"Aleera, are you well?" asked Jaxson.

She shook her head. "Yes. And yes, I can pick locks. We need to hurry."

"I can help you with the chain," said Tam. "Jaxson, you and Zero do your stuff."

Jaxson approached the injured dragon slowly, his hands held out, sending out calm thoughts. Zero walked to the other side.

"The dragon knows we are here to help," said Zero.

"Let's get to it, then."

Jaxson placed both hands near to the long wound on the dragon's side. Zero placed a wing over the dragon's back. Jaxson extended his mind to Zero. The hair on the back of Jaxson's neck stood as Zero gathered energy and held it. Then his fingertips started to tingle as Zero slowly released the energy, through the other dragon, to Jaxson. Jaxson's arms buzzed with energy, then his whole body, until he was about to burst with the magic contained within him. He concentrated and willed it to flow back to Zero. The wound on the dragon's side closed until only a thin, red line of a scar remained.

The healed dragon lifted its head, then stood slowly. The heavy chain that Tam and Aleera had been struggling with fell away. It unfurled his wings and stretched its neck out. The purple scales along its back shimmered as the dragon shook out the stiffness from being held captive by the restraints.

It turned to Jaxson and then to Zero. Finally, it looked at Aleera as she stepped forward.

"*She* says thank you, and her name is Soaren," said Aleera with a blank face.

Jaxson's eyes widened. "Amazing! I've never met a female dragon and.... you can hear her?"

Aleera simply nodded and placed a hand on Soaren's head. Tears fell down her face, and her body shook. Tam's eyes were wide; he was clearly as shocked as Jaxson.

A voice from behind them brought everyone out of their surprised stupors.

"Jaxson? What are you doing here?" said a tall man wearing the uniform of the DLDC and holding a large ring of keys.

"Dad?!"

CHAPTER 37

Jaxson thought back to the last time he had seen his father. The early spring dew was on the grass as the sun crested over the Dragon Spine Mountains. There was a chill in the air that warned that winter may have one more storm to send their way. They were outside the cabin, and his father was dressed for traveling. It had been a great three months, but like always, his dad had a job that needed doing. Jaxson sat on the big rock beside the cabin, with Zero right behind him, and watched his dad disappear along the path that led west into Crystal Forge.

Now, here he was, right in front of him. Just as Jaxson had agreed the search was less important than the life of the captured dragon, his father had appeared. But he was wearing the uniform of the Demon Lizard Death Cult. Something gnawed at the back of Jaxson's mind.

"Jaxson, you can't be here," said Alan. Then he noticed Zero near the gate. "For all the tiny gods' tears, Zero's here too! Out, now! Even I can't protect you in here."

Tam stepped forward. "It's him. The one I told you about. He's their leader!"

Jaxson looked back and forth between his dad and Tam. His mouth hung open and his eyes lost focus. "What the…"

"It doesn't matter right now," said Alan. "You have to go. All of you."

Aleera didn't have to be told again. Quickly, she was on Soaren's back, and they disappeared out of the gate. Jaxson saw the purple dragon rising and then banking to the east.

Tam stepped in between Jaxson and his father. "Jaxson, get

on Zero and get out of here. We have what we came for," he said, pulling out his short sword.

"Listen to your friend," said Alan.

Jaxson started to object, but Tam pushed him toward Zero. The dragon nudged him gently with his head, and Jaxson climbed into the harness just as a score of soldiers broke down the door. Alan's eyes widened as he saw them stream into the room. He shouted, "Rebels! They released the dragon. Take them alive – I'll have questions for them to answer."

Zero didn't give them the chance. He was through the gate and in the air before the soldiers took another step.

Jaxson looked back over his shoulder to see Tam surrounded, his sword still ready. He feared his friend wouldn't be taken without a fight. The next moment, they were too high to see Tam any longer. Jaxson scanned the skies for signs of Aleera and Soaren. Then it struck him that Aleera and Soaren were like Zero and him. He didn't know how it had happened, but it was true. But in the darkness, he couldn't see them anywhere.

Dragon's fire lit the sky to the west. Dreknoxious and Tollison were still causing a ruckus. Jaxson thought he caught a glimpse of a purple dragon headed south, away from the city. He hoped it was Aleera and Soaren escaping, even if it was in the wrong direction.

"Stick to the plan. Circle wide over the Laguza and head back to Mount Fornessor," said Jaxson.

Zero didn't respond right away; he simply flew faster and higher, away from the keep.

"Perhaps Aleera is going to circle to the Mount from the south," said Zero.

"Maybe. More than likely, she'll go wherever Soaren leads her. It's what I would do in her place," replied Jaxson.

"Do you want to talk about your father?" asked Zero.

"Yes. But not now. We need to get somewhere safe."

They flew farther north than they had ever been, through the night and into the early morning sun. Somewhere over the Laguza Sea, when Jaxson thought they were in the clear, Blackthorn and his rider, Grayton, crashed into them, hard.

CHAPTER 38

Zero tumbled toward the sea below. Jaxson gripped the harness with every bit of strength he possessed, and even that was barely enough. Just before splashing down into the sea, Zero righted himself and flew straight across the surface of the water, gaining altitude with each beat of his wings. As he reached for his bow, Jaxson spotted Blackthorn high above them, keeping pace. He nocked an arrow, and Zero banked hard right. Blackthorn shifted, then dove down towards Zero once again.

This time, however, Jaxson warned Zero, who was able to turn away without taking the full impact of the black dragon's strike. Still, he took a mighty blow just behind his rear legs. Blackthorn was above them again in moments. Each time Zero veered one way or the other, their enemy mirrored him. The islands in the distance were too far away to be of any help. There was no cover over the flat water.

"We have to change this up. We are at his mercy down here," shouted Jaxson.

"*Take the shot at Grayton this time,*" said Zero. "*Whatever happens, take the shot, and do not miss.*" He angled toward the islands and slowed down, feigning a more severe injury than he actually had.

Blackthorn dove, but stopped short of impact and flew directly above them, just out of bow range. Grayton's head appeared over the black dragon's shoulder, smiled wickedly, and yelled, "I see you boy! Nowhere to run to now."

Just as his laughter reached Jaxson, Blackthorn dove sharply. Zero waited until the last possible moment, then turned and flew straight up, exposing his vulnerable underbelly but giving Jaxson a clear shot. The arrow was at Jaxson's ear and released before he even realized it.

A scream of pain from Grayton let Jaxson know he was on target but had missed a fatal shot.

Blackthorn abandoned the attack and whirled away. Jaxson let out a whoop as the bounty hunter retreated.

"*I need to rest,*" said Zero.

"Head for the islands. I think we bought ourselves some time," said Jaxson.

****

From the top of the ruined tower on the deserted island Jaxson and Zero had a commanding view in all directions. No one would be able to approach without being seen. It gave them time to address Zero's wound and make a new plan.

"What's next?" asked Jaxson as he cleaned the last of the blood from Zero's back.

"*Perhaps Aleera or Dreknoxious have already arrived at Mount Fornessor. We should go there as the original plan dictated.*"

"That's one option," said Jaxson. "But we need to find a way to get Tam out. There's no way he could have fought his way through all of those soldiers. He was definitely captured, or worse."

"*If he was captured, he may have revealed our destination. Mount Fornessor may not be the best place to go,*"

Zero gestured with his head, indicating for Jaxson to look back in the direction from which they had come. Dragons were flying directly above the water, slowly weaving back and forth. They were searching for Zero and him. Grayton must have told them of Zero's injury.

"How many do you count?"

"*There are three searching the water and one well above,*" replied Zero. "*It might be Blackthorn, though I cannot be sure at this distance.*"

Jaxson sighed. He didn't want to leave, even though that was the safest course of action. It would mean going away from Tam, his only friend. Away from Aleera and Soaren, a pair like him and Zero. Away from the father he had sought for so long. Away from the only connections he had in life, other than Zero. He simply had no idea what came next.

"What do we do now?"

A familiar voice came from behind them. "First, I think you need to tell me exactly what happened."

Both Jaxson and Zero started violently before turning to see Dreknoxious standing near to the edge of the ruins.

"Where did you come from?

CHAPTER 39

"Are you hurt? No? Good. Let's have a look at Zero then, shall we?"

Dreknoxious wasted little time in assessing the wound on Zero's back. Jaxson had cleaned it well, and the old man gave him a nod of approval.

"It's so frustrating that we can heal others but not ourselves," said Jaxson. Dreknoxious raised an eyebrow and Jaxson shrugged. "I do have some secrets, you know."

Dreknoxious snorted. "Not as many as you might think. Now, tell me what happened."

Jaxson launched into the tale of the daring rescue the previous night. He left nothing out. When he recounted the part about Aleera and Soaren, Dreknoxious interrupted, guessing what had happened next. The old man appeared very excited that Aleera had bonded with the dragon, but he didn't seem surprised. Then Jaxson had to tell the part about his dad's betrayal. His eyes burned, and his stomach rolled violently as if a rabbit was hopping around in there.

Dreknoxious allowed Jaxson to release all of his pent-up emotions, then pulled him into a strong embrace as Jaxson sobbed. Suddenly, Jaxson remembered the dragons and bounty hunters that were searching for them. He pushed himself away from Dreknoxious and searched the skies.

"What are you looking for, Jaxson?" asked the old man.

"We saw some dragons searching for us, just before you showed up," replied Jaxson. "I just don't want to be surprised again."

"They are gone."

NOTHING MORE THAN ZERO

"How do you know?" asked Jaxson with a frown.

"Because I told the dragons they needed to search elsewhere," replied Dreknoxious. "So they did."

After some hesitation, Jaxson stammered, "Who are you? Really? I know you were dad's friend, but who are you?"

"Perhaps it is time you know. You are going to be stronger and more important than me soon, anyway," said Dreknoxious. "I am the last remaining Wizard of Greeti, and I have long awaited the day that dragonriders once more rule the skies with might and magic. Finally, the day is near. Who I am is not as important as who you will become... Dragonrider Jaxson."

EPILOGUE

Zero stood beside Jaxson as they looked into the portal within the Temple of Greeti inside the Taufan. The ancient dragon, Forseti, stood near to the end of the long hall, eagerly waiting to see whether the young dragon and his dragonrider would brave the portal in search of the tools needed to reach their potential. He had not been surprised when they had returned days ago. It had been quicker than he anticipated, but there was never any doubt they would return.

Forseti had told them they needed training if they were to become dragon and rider together, for Jaxson to become a dragonrider. He explained there was no one alive that could guide them, but there was a way to gain the necessary training. Through the portal, they could enter the land of their ancestors and seek a book – a book that, if read correctly, would help them prepare for the journey ahead. They did not know it, though Forseti thought Zero had an idea, but their destinies were intertwined not only with each other but with the destiny of the whole of Kealqua.

Zero looked at Forseti before turning back to the portal. As one, Jaxson and his dragon stepped forward into the shimmering void. Then they were gone, and Forseti sighed. It had begun. There was a chance.

"It is done, then?" asked Dreknoxious as he materialized beside Forseti.

"It is as you said it would be," replied Forseti. "But is it the way it should be?"

"You know what we face. We need dragonriders," said the old man.

"Need them? It is because of them we are in this position to begin with, but you are too young to have experienced that," said Forseti.

"I am old... But you are right. Too young for that," sighed Dreknoxious.

"Will he find it?"

Dreknoxious thought back to all he knew of Jaxson, Zero, and Alan, Jaxson's father. "I would be surprised if he did not. He has a great ally in Zero – his only ally, really. But people do the most unlikely things at times. Still, the only reason he agreed to go is because he *felt* isolated, alone. He had nothing left here. Nothing more than Zero."

"You saw to that," said Forseti.

"I did what I thought I must," said Dreknoxious. "Now it is up to Jaxson and Zero to bring back the knowledge we need. I think he will succeed. He has to... Or the world as we know it will cease to exist."

SPECIAL THANKS

A person could search from the Shire to Crystal Forge and everywhere in-between and not find a more supportive wife than mine. Thank you, Tara, for letting me chase this dream.

My Mama and my sister, two of my best cheerleaders, deserve a big thank you for keeping me motivated and engaged. And my Dad, thanks for believing in me.

Ashley, the best sister-in-law ever, thank you for the constant support and doing a final read through. I hope you are interested in helping with the next one.

ABOUT THE AUTHOR

C. H. Smith

C. H. Smith is an American author currently residing in Texas. He has lived in several of the southeastern states soaking up the culture of each one. Family and friends are of the utmost importance to him, and he seeks to show their value in everything he writes.

Having a passion for reading and hearing stories has led to a lifetime of enjoyment and adventure inside the pages of classics, fantasy, and engaging short stories.

C.H. earned his BA in English from Belhaven College in Jackson, MS although he has not put it to use. After a career selling fishing lures ended, he decided to tell the stories that have long rattled around in his head.

BOOKS BY THIS AUTHOR

The Princess Knight

I knew the sad man at the bar had a story he needed to tell. At the time, I didn't realize that I needed to hear it just as much.

As he began, Daniel weaved a tale of a princess's quest to counter a sorcerer's vile curse. She traveled across the whole kingdom with her talking canine companion, making new friends and battling fearsome enemies the whole way. The stakes were high in the magical story he told, and it didn't take long to realize, the stakes were higher in the real world his tale mirrored.

Hearing the story would change me forever…

Made in the USA
Middletown, DE
08 January 2023

21651587R00080